Before
we
were Free

julia alvarez

Alfred A. Knopf

NEW YORK

THIS IS A BORZOI BOOK PUBLISHED BY ALFRED A. KNOPF

Text copyright © 2002 by Julia Alvarez

Jacket illustration copyright © 1975 by Edward G. Acker III

Map illustrations by Lisa Paterno Guinta

All rights reserved under International and Pan-American Copyright Conventions. Published in the United States by Alfred A. Knopf, a division of Random House, Inc., New York, and simultaneously in Canada by Random House of Canada Limited, Toronto. Distributed by Random House, Inc., New York.

www.randomhouse.com/teens

KNOPF, BORZOI BOOKS, and the colophon are registered trademarks of Random House, Inc.

Library of Congress Cataloging-in-Publication Data

Alvarez, Julia.

Before we were free / Julia Alvarez

p.   cm.

Summary: In the early 1960s in the Dominican Republic, twelve-year-old Anita learns that her family is involved in the underground movement to end the bloody rule of the dictator, General Trujillo.

ISBN 0-375-81544-9 (trade) — ISBN 0-375-91544-3 (lib. bdg.)

1. Dominican Republic—History—1930–1961—Juvenile fiction. [1. Dominican Republic—History—1930–1961—Fiction. 2. Family life—Dominican Republic—Fiction. 3. Revolutions—Fiction. 4. Trujillo Molina, Rafael Leânidas, 1891–1961—Fiction. 5. Dominican Republic—Fiction.] I. Title.

PZ7.A48 Be 2002

[Fic]—dc21   2001050520

Printed in the United States of America

August 2002

10 9 8 7 6 5 4 3 2 1

First Edition

for those who stayed

contents

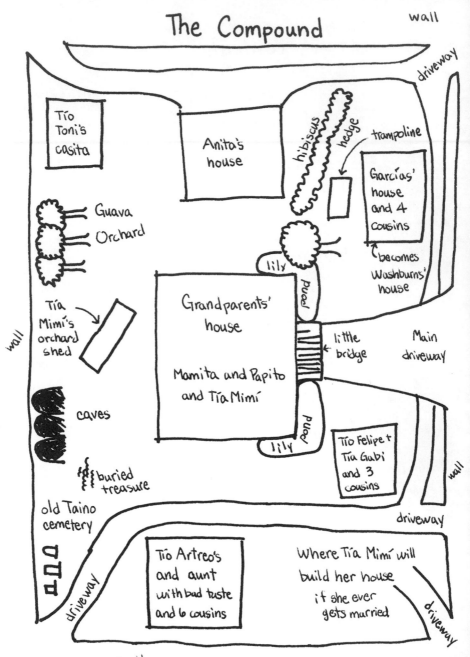

The Compound

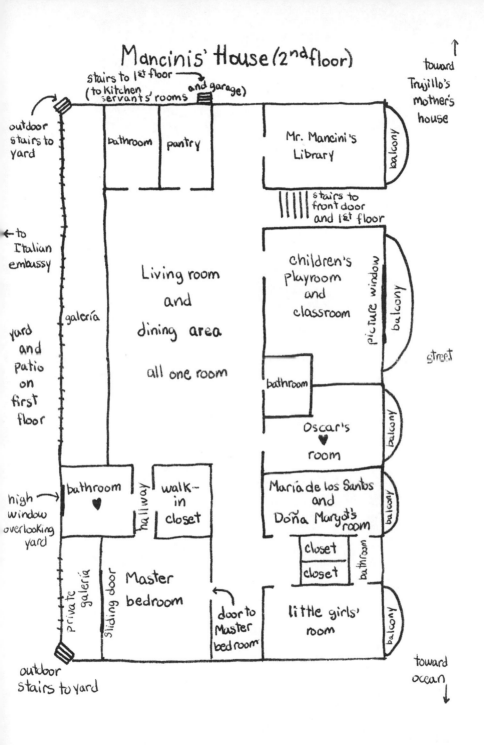

one

The Eraser in the Shape of the Dominican Republic

"May I have some volunteers?" Mrs. Brown is saying. We are preparing skits for Thanksgiving, two weeks away. Although the Pilgrims never came to the Dominican Republic, we are attending the American school, so we have to celebrate American holidays.

It's a hot, muggy afternoon. I feel lazy and bored. Outside the window, the palm trees are absolutely still. Not even a breeze. Some of the American students have been complaining that it doesn't feel like Thanksgiving when it's as hot as the Fourth of July.

Mrs. Brown is looking around the room. My cousin, Carla, sits in the seat in front of me, waving her arm.

Mrs. Brown calls on Carla, and then on me. Carla and I are to play the parts of two Indians welcoming the Pilgrims. Mrs. Brown always gives the not-so-good parts to those of us in class who are Dominicans.

She hands us each a headband with a feather sticking up like one rabbit ear. I feel ridiculous. "Okay, Indians, come forward and greet the Pilgrims." Mrs. Brown motions toward where Joey Farland and Charlie Price stand with their toy rifles and the Davy Crockett hats they've talked Mrs. Brown into letting them wear. Even I know the pioneers come after the Pilgrims.

"Anita"—she points at me—"I want you to say, 'Welcome to the United States.' "

Before I can mutter my line, Oscar Mancini raises his hand. "Why the Indians call it the United Estates when there was no United Estates back then, Mrs. Brown?"

The class groans. Oscar is always asking questions. "United Estates! United Estates!" somebody in the back row mimics. Lots of classmates snicker, even some Dominicans. I hate it when the American kids make fun of the way we speak English.

"That's a good question, Oscar," Mrs. Brown responds, casting a disapproving look around. She must have heard the whisper as well. "It's called poetic license. Something allowed in a story that isn't so in real life. Like a metaphor or a simile."

Just then, the classroom door opens. I catch a glimpse of our principal, and behind him, Carla's mother, Tía Laura, looking very nervous. But then, Tía Laura always looks nervous. Papi likes to joke that if there were ever an Olympic event for worrying, the Dominican Republic would win with his sister on the team. But lately, Papi looks pretty worried himself. When I ask questions, he replies with "Children should be seen, not heard" instead of his usual "Curiosity is a sign of intelligence."

Mrs. Brown comes forward from the back of the room and stands talking to the principal for a minute before she follows him out into the hall, where Tía Laura is standing. The door closes.

Usually when our teacher leaves the room, Charlie Price, the class clown, acts up. He does stuff like changing the hands on the clock so that Mrs. Brown will be all confused and let us out for recess early. Yesterday, he wrote NO HOMEWORK TONIGHT in big block letters above the date on the board, THURSDAY, NOVEMBER 10, 1960. Even Mrs. Brown thought that was pretty funny.

But now the whole class waits quietly. The last time the principal came to our classroom, it was to tell Tomasito Morales that his mother was here for him. Something had happened to his father, but even Papi, who knew Señor Morales, would not say what. Tomasito hasn't come back to school since then.

Beside me, Carla is tucking her hair behind her ears, something she does when she's nervous. My brother, Mundín, has a nervous tic, too. He bites his nails whenever he does something wrong and has to sit on the punishment chair until Papi comes home.

The door opens again, and Mrs. Brown steps back in, smiling that phony smile grown-ups smile when they are keeping bad news from you. In a bright voice, Mrs. Brown asks Carla to please collect her things. "Would you help her, Anita?" she adds.

We walk back to our seats and begin packing up Carla's school-bag. Mrs. Brown announces to the class that they'll continue with their skits later. Everyone is to take out his or her vocabulary book and start on the next chapter. The class pretends to settle down to its work, but of course, everyone is stealing glances at Carla and me.

Mrs. Brown comes over to see how we're doing. Carla packs her homework, but leaves the usual stay-at-school stuff in her desk.

"Are those yours?" Mrs. Brown points at the new notebooks, the neat lineup of pens and pencils, the eraser in the shape of the Dominican Republic.

Carla nods.

"Pack it all up, dear," Mrs. Brown says quietly.

We pack Carla's schoolbag with everything that belongs to her. The whole time I'm wondering why Mrs. Brown hasn't asked me to pack my stuff, too. After all, Carla and I are in the same family.

Oscar's hand is waving and dipping like a palm tree in a cyclone. But Mrs. Brown doesn't call on him. This time, I think we're all hoping he'll get a chance to ask his question, which is probably the same question that's in everyone's head: Where is Carla going?

Mrs. Brown takes Carla's hand. "Come along." She nods to me.

Mrs. Brown leads Carla up the side of the classroom. I follow, afraid I'll burst into tears if I catch anyone's eye. I look up at the portrait of our Benefactor, El Jefe, which hangs above the class-room, his eyes watching over us. To his left hangs George Wash-ington in his white wig, looking off into the distance. Perhaps he is homesick for his own country?

Just staring at El Jefe keeps my tears from flowing. I want to be brave and strong, so that someday if I ever meet the leader of our country, he'll congratulate me. "So, you are the girl who never cries?" he'll say, smiling down at me.

As we cross the front of the class, Mrs. Brown turns to make sure I'm behind her. She reaches and I take the free hand she is holding out to me.

We ride home in the Garcías' Plymouth with the silver fins that remind me of the shark I saw at the beach last summer. I'm stuffed in the back with Carla and her younger sisters, Sandi and Yo, who've been taken out of their classes, too. A silent and worried-looking Tía Laura sits in front next to Papi, who is driving.

"What's happening?" I keep asking. "Is something wrong?"

"*Cotorrita,*" Papi warns playfully. That's my nickname in the family because sometimes I talk too much, like a little parrot, Mami says. But then at school, I'm the total opposite and Mrs. Brown complains that I need to speak up more.

Papi begins explaining that the Garcías have finally gotten per-mission to leave the country, and they'll be taking the airplane in a few hours to go to the United States of America. He's trying to sound excited, looking in the rearview mirror at us. "You'll get to see the snow!"

None of the García sisters says a word.

"And Papito and Mamita and all your cousins," Papi goes on. "Isn't that so, Laura?"

"Sí, sí, sí," Tía Laura agrees. She sounds like someone letting air out of a tire.

My grandparents left for New York at the beginning of September. My other aunts and uncles were already there, having gone away with the younger cousins back in June. Who knows where Tío Toni is? Now, with the García cousins leaving, only my family will be left living at the compound.

I lean forward with my arms on the front seat. "So are we going to go, too, Papi?"

Papi shakes his head. "Somebody has to stay and mind the store." That's what he always says whenever he can't go on an outing because he has to work. Papito, my grandfather, started Construcciones de la Torre, a concrete-block business to build houses that won't blow over during hurricanes. When my grandfather retired a few years ago, Papi, being the oldest, was put in charge.

As we come up the driveway to the García house, I see Mami and Lucinda and Mundín waiting for us. Somebody must have picked up my older sister and brother at the high school so they can say good-bye to the Garcías, too. Behind them stands Chucha, our old nanny, in her long purple dress, holding my baby cousin, Fifi, in her arms.

As soon as the car doors open, I run to Mami, who puts her arms around me. She doesn't have to ask me what's wrong. A row of suitcases have been brought out and lined up, ready to be loaded into the car. Beside them stands Mr. Washburn, a tall, skinny man with a bow tie that makes his whole face look like a gift someone wrapped up real nice. Papi has explained that Mr. Washburn is the American consul, who represents the United States when Ambassador Farland is out of the country.

"Troops all here?" he asks cheerily. "Ready to go?"

"Where's Papi?" Yo asks. She and I are the Oscars of our family, always asking questions. But I don't always get to ask mine when Yo is around.

A look passes from one adult to another as if they are playing musical chairs with their eyes, trying to decide who'll be the one stuck answering Yo's question. Finally, Papi speaks up. "He'll be waiting for you at the airport."

It seems rude of Tío Carlos not to say good-bye. But something so unusual is going on that good manners seem beside the point.

"Okay, girls," Tía Laura says, clapping her hands. "I want you to go to your rooms and change into the clothes on your bed. Chucha'll go with you." Tía Laura takes baby Fifi from Chucha's hands so that the old woman will be free to help the girls.

"Do we bring our bookbags with us?" Yo wants to know.

Tía Laura shakes her head. "One special thing, just one each, girls. We can only take ten kilos apiece."

"Can Anita come and help me pick?" Carla asks. She has already taken my hand and is leading me away with her.

"Just be sure you make it quick!" Tía Laura scolds, but even her scolding voice has nothing but worry in it.

The bedroom the girls share has a long closet down one side of it. The sliding door has been rolled back and many of the drawers are gaping open with clothes hanging out. Whoever packed did so in a hurry.

Carla's eyes sweep over a high shelf where toys and trinkets are stored out of the way. Three ballerina jewelry boxes stand open, the little dancers with their arms over their heads. Behind them, the hula hoops are lined up, each one a different color so the girls won't fight.

"I just can't decide," Carla admits. She seems on the verge of tears, tucking stray hair behind her ears.

"Girls!" we hear their mother calling from the hall.

"What do I choose?" Carla asks me desperately, as if I know what she'll need in the United States of America, where I've never been.

"Your jewelry box," I suggest. It'll be a way to take more than one thing. The box is filled with Carla's bangles and her butterfly pin and her chain with a little cross—jewelry that isn't real gold.

Carla nods agreement. As I climb up on a chair, my eye is caught by a snow globe with the tiny deer nibbling the ground. I can't resist giving it a shake, stirring up the snowstorm until I cannot see the little deer.

"That's mine," Yo cries out, reaching her hands for it. "That's what I'm taking."

"That's so stupid, Yo," Carla scolds. She rolls her eyes at me as if the two of us know better than to take a snow globe to a place where there's already going to be snow.

"You're the stupid one!" Yo shoots back.

Soon the two of them are shouting. It doesn't take much to get two García girls arguing. Their raised voices draw their mother to the room.

"If I hear another word, I'm going to leave you all here and go to New York by myself!" she threatens. "Now choose what you want and change into your clothes. The car's ready for us."

There is no more fooling around. On each bed there's a petticoat and party dress ready to be put on. The girls dress quickly.

Out in the driveway, Mr. Washburn is already sitting in his big black car with the little American flag on the antenna. Papi leans against the passenger side, talking to him through the open window.

"We're keeping Mr. Washburn waiting," Tía Laura scolds. She nudges the girls to say their good-byes.

Suddenly, Yo announces, "I don't want to go. I want to stay with Tía Carmen."

That starts a chain reaction. "Me too," Sandi sobs, clinging to my mother. In Tía Laura's arms, Fifi begins bawling, reaching her chubby little hands for Chucha, who stands at the door with her arms crossed. I feel like crying, too, but I know Mami is counting on me to cheer up the García girls.

"Girls, please, I can't take this right now," Tía Laura begins, but then she, too, bursts into tears.

Papi hurries over to his sister's side. He puts his arm around her, speaking softly, the way he speaks to me when I've had a nightmare.

"Come here, girls." Mami gathers the García sisters around her, squatting down so she can talk to them privately. "You go along with your mami and behave yourselves, please. We'll be seeing you soon, I promise!"

I'm surprised. Papi has said we have to stay and mind the store. So it must be that the Garcías are just going away for a short trip.

My cousins seem comforted by this news. For a moment it

crosses my mind that maybe Mami is just saying this to make them feel better. Like telling my grandmother in *Nueva York* that Tío Toni is fine, so Mamita won't worry about my young uncle, whom we haven't seen in months.

Mr. Washburn pops his head out of the car and says, "Time to go, folks!" The García girls go down the line, hugging and kissing each of us. They've already set their special toys on the backseat of the car. Through the open door, I can see Yo's snow globe, the storm starting to settle down so the tiny deer can eat the flakes strewn on the ground.

When Carla gets to me, the tears well up in my eyes. I can't help it. There's no portrait of El Jefe out here to make me brave and strong. I hang my head as the tears drop down.

"We'll see you soon," Carla reminds me. But it only makes me cry harder when she reaches over and absently pushes my hair back behind my ears.

After the car leaves, we stand for a while looking down the empty driveway. I feel hollow inside, as if a big part of me is gone. Finally, we turn and cross over to our house through the hibiscus hedge, carrying the bookbags of supplies the García girls left for us to use.

Overnight, we've become what Mrs. Brown calls a nuclear family, just my parents and my sister and brother, instead of the large *familia* of uncles and aunts and cousins and my grandparents, who were living in the compound only a few months ago. Now all the houses but ours are empty. The orchid shed is full of straggly blossoms. The hammock that used to hang in the porch of Tío Toni's bachelor pad has been taken down. The pond is overrun with bullfrogs that croak all night long.

For the rest of the afternoon, I mope around the house, until Mami sends me over to help Chucha move in. Chucha has been part of our family for as long as anyone can remember and has taken care of every baby since Papi was born. In fact, Chucha took care of me, too, as she likes to remind me. "You're never too old to mind me," she'll say. "After all, I was the one who changed your diapers." What a thing to be reminded of! At least she's nice enough never to bring it up in public.

First thing we move over is Chucha's coffin. Porfirio, the gardener, balances it across the wheelbarrow, and Chucha and I walk on either side, holding on to each end. I know it's pretty strange, but this is Chucha's bed she sleeps in every night! She says she wants to prepare herself for the next life. Chucha's people came from Haiti, where they do things different from us.

Inside the coffin, we've packed up all her purple clothes. That's another thing. Chucha always wears purple because she once made a promise that she would always wear purple. But she's never said why she made such a promise or to whom or why she decided on purple. Yellow or even lavender would be a lot more cheerful.

Chucha also has dreams where she can see the future. Mundín likes to say, "You would, too, if you slept in a coffin!" As a matter of fact, a few weeks ago, Chucha dreamed that my cousins would be leaving for a city of tall buildings before my cousins even knew they would be leaving for New York.

Strange as Chucha is, I'm glad she's moving in with us. I feel safer when she's around. And now especially with everyone gone, it'll be comforting to have Chucha in our house.

"Chucha," I ask her after we've moved all her things over, "how soon do you think I'll see the Garcías?"

Chucha narrows her shiny eyes. Her wrinkled black face wrinkles even more when she concentrates. She doesn't say anything for a while. Then she looks straight at me and says one of her riddles: "You will see them before they come back but only after you are free."

I feel too scared to ask her when that might possibly be.

At supper, Papi explains that the construction business isn't doing all that well, that we're going to have to economize, that the *familia* is going to be scattered for a while—

"For how long?" I want to know.

Mami gives me her warning look that reminds me that I am interrupting. Little parrot or not, I am almost twelve and have to learn some manners.

Suddenly, a black moth flaps into the room. Talk about interrupting! It's as big as my hand. "A bat!" Lucinda screams, and ducks under the table.

"It's not a bat. It's a black butterfly," Mundín observes, leaping up to catch it.

"Don't touch it!" Mami cries. We all know from Chucha that a black moth is an omen of death. Mundín stops in his tracks. The moth lifts off and disappears into the night.

"You can come out now, Lucinda," Mami calls in a teasing voice. But she looks pretty shaky herself.

Lucinda rises slowly from under the table. Tears are rolling down her face. "This place is just . . . just . . . just . . . so . . . sad," she sobs, then storms out of the room.

Mami and Papi exchange a tense look. Papi stands up from his place at the table. As he goes by me, he plants a kiss on top of my head. "My grown-up baby girl," he says.

I feel proud to be acting more mature than Lucinda, but the truth is, I'm just as sad even if I'm not showing it.

After supper, I try tidying my room to make myself feel better. But when I empty the contents of Carla's schoolbag on my bed— her neatly sharpened pencils, her notebooks with pictures of kittens tangled in balls of yarn, her funny eraser that she got for winning the recitation contest on Independence Day last February—I feel the sadness stir up again like a storm inside me. There's no way I'll be able to use my cousin's supplies. I pack everything back in her bag and stick it in my closet. Or so I think. A little later, I crawl into bed and jump right back out. I've felt something hard, a cockroach or scorpion, under the covers. But when Chucha draws back the sheets, we find the eraser in the shape of the Dominican Republic.

two

¡Shhh!

The day after my cousins leave, Papi goes to work early, taking Mundín with him. Now that none of my uncles are around, Papi has a lot more to do at the office.

I'm alone at the breakfast table, already feeling how long and lonely this Saturday is going to be without Carla. Chucha and Mami and Ursulina, the cook, are in the kitchen, discussing what's needed at the market. Lucinda is still sleeping her beauty sleep that will last all morning long. Outside, Porfirio is watering the ginger plants, singing a Mexican song.

The woman I love ran off with another—
I followed their footsteps and murdered them both.

What a cheerful start to my day! I'm thinking when, suddenly, Porfirio stops singing. I glance out the window.

A half-dozen black Volkswagens are crawling up our driveway.

Before the cars come to a complete stop, the doors open, and a stream of men pour out all over the property. In their dark glasses, they look like gangsters in the American movies that sometimes come to town.

I run to get Mami, but she's already headed for the door. Four men stand in our entryway, all dressed in khaki pants with small holsters at their belts and tiny revolvers that don't look real. The head guy—or at least he does all the talking—asks Mami for Carlos García and his family. I know something is really wrong when Mami says, "Why? Aren't they home?"

But then, instead of going away, this guy asks if his men can search our house. Mami, who I'm sure will say, "Do you have a *permiso?*" steps aside like the toilet is overflowing and these are the plumbers coming to the rescue!

I trail behind Mami. "Who are they?" I ask.

Mami swings around, a terrified look on her face, and hisses, "Not now!"

I race to find Chucha, who's in the entryway, shaking her head at the muddy boot prints. I ask her who these strange men are.

"SIM," she whispers. She makes a creepy gesture of cutting off her head with her index finger.

"But *who* are the SIM?" I ask again. I'm feeling more and more panicked at how nobody is giving me a straight answer.

"*Policía secreta,*" she explains. "They go around investigating everyone and then disappearing them."

"*Secret* police?"

Chucha gives me her long, slow, guillotine nod that cuts off any further questions.

They go from room to room, looking in every nook and cranny.

When they come through the hall door to the bedroom part of the house, Mami hesitates. "Just a routine search, *doña,*" the head guy says. Mami smiles wanly, trying to show she has nothing to hide.

In my room, one guy lifts the baby-doll pajamas I left lying on the floor as if a secret weapon is hidden underneath. Another yanks the covers back from my bed. I hold on tight to Mami's ice-cold hand and she tightens her hold on mine.

The men go into Lucinda's room without knocking, opening up the jalousies, lifting the bedskirt and matching skirt on her vanity, plunging their bayonets underneath. My older sister sits up in bed, startled, her pink-foam rollers askew from sleeping on them. A horrible red rash has broken out on her neck.

When the men are done searching the room, Mami gives Lucinda and me her look that means business. "I want you both in here while I accompany our visitors," she says with strained politeness.

I run to her side. "Mami, no!" I start wailing. I don't want her to go with these creepy policemen. What if they hurt her?

The head guy turns to me. With his dark glasses on, I can't see his eyes, only the reflection of a terrified girl clinging to her mother. "What are you crying about, eh? *¡Tranquila!*" he orders.

It's as if his steely command cuts off the breath in my lungs. I can't even move when Mami gently undoes my hands from around her waist. She follows the men out, pulling the door closed behind her.

Lucinda turns to me. She's scratching the rash on her neck, even though Mami has told her not to. "What is going on?"

"Chucha said they're secret police," I tell her. "They were asking for the Garcías, but Mami acted like she didn't know." My voice breaks when I think of Mami all alone with them right this moment.

"The SIM know perfectly well where the Garcías are," Lucinda says. "They just want an excuse to traipse through here. And of course, they'd love to get their hands on Papi."

"But why?"

Lucinda looks at me as if I'm a lot dumber than she thought I was. "Don't you know anything, Anita?" Her eyes stray up to my hair. "You've got to do something with those bangs," she says, brushing them back with her hand. It's the closest she can come to saying something nice when she sees how scared I am.

Lucinda and I wait in her room, listening at the door, tense with concentration. When we don't hear noises anymore, Lucinda turns the knob carefully, and we tiptoe out into the hall.

The SIM seem to have left. We spot Chucha crossing the patio toward the front of the house, a broom over her shoulder like a rifle. She looks like she's going to shoot the SIM for tracking mud on her clean floors.

"Chucha!" We wave to her to come talk to us.

"Where's Mami?" I ask, feeling the same mounting panic I felt earlier when Mami left with the SIM. "Is she okay?"

"She's on the *teléfono*, calling Don Mundo," Chucha explains.

"What about . . . ?" Lucinda wrinkles her nose instead of saying their names.

"*Esos animales*," Chucha says, shaking her head. Those animals, the SIM, searched every house in the compound, getting more and more destructive when they didn't find what they were looking for, tromping through Chucha's room, turning over her coffin and tearing off the velvet lining. They also stormed through Porfirio's and Ursulina's rooms. "Those two are so terrified," Chucha concludes, "they are packing their things and leaving the house."

But the SIM stay. They sit in their black Volkswagens at the top of our drive, blocking our way out.

At dinner, Papi says everything will be fine. We just have to act as if the SIM aren't there and carry on with normal life. But I notice that, like the rest of us, he doesn't eat a single bite. And is it really normal that Mami and Papi have us all sleep on mattresses on their bedroom floor with the door locked?

We lie in the dark, talking in whispers, Mundín on a mat by himself, Lucinda and I on a larger mattress, and Papi and Mami on theirs they placed right beside ours.

"How come you don't just stay up on your bed?" I ask.

"Keep your voice down," Mami reminds me.

"Okay, okay," I whisper. But I still don't get an answer. "And what about Chucha?" I ask. "She's all by herself at the back of the house."

"Don't worry," Mundín says, "I don't think a bullet can get through that coffin!"

"Bullets!" I sit right up in bed.

"Shhhh!" my whole family reminds me.

Those black cars sit there for days and days—sometimes there's only one, sometimes as many as three. Every morning, when Papi leaves for the office, one of the cars starts up its colicky motor and follows him down the hill. In the evening, when he comes home, it comes back with him. I don't know when those SIM ever go to their own houses to eat their suppers and talk with their kids.

"Are they really policemen?" I keep asking Mami. It doesn't make any sense. If the SIM are policemen, secret or not, shouldn't we trust them instead of being afraid of them? But all Mami will say is "Shhh!" Meanwhile, we can't go to school because something might happen to us. "Like what?" I ask. Like what Chucha said about people disappearing? Is that what Mami worries will happen to us? "Didn't Papi say we should carry on with normal life?"

"Anita, *por favor*," Mami pleads, collapsing in a hall chair. She leans forward and whispers in my ear, "Please, please, you must stop asking questions."

"But why?" I whisper back. I can smell her shampoo, which smells like coconuts in her hair.

"Because I don't have any answers," she replies.

Not that Mami is the only one I try talking to.

My brother, Mundín, who's two years older, sometimes explains things to me. But this time when I ask him what's going on, he looks worried and whispers, "Ask Papi." He's biting his nails again, something he stopped doing when he turned fourteen in August.

I try asking Papi.

One evening when the phone rings, I follow him into our living room. I hear him say something about some butterflies in a car accident.

"Butterflies in a car accident?" I ask, puzzled.

He seems startled that I'm in the room. "What are you doing here?" he snaps.

I put my hands on my hips. "Honestly, Papi! I live here!" I can't believe he's asking me what I'm doing in our own living room! Of course, he immediately apologizes. "Sorry, *amorcito,* you startled me." His eyes are moist, as if he's holding back tears.

"So what about those butterflies, Papi?"

"They're not real butterflies," he explains softly. "It's just . . . a nickname for some very special ladies who had an . . . accident last night."

"What kind of an accident? And why are they called butterflies anyhow? Don't they have a real name?"

Again a *shhh*.

My last resort is asking Lucinda. My older sister has been in a vile mood since the SIM cornered us in our own house. Lucinda loves parties and talking on the phone, and she hates being cooped up. She spends most of the time in her room, trying out so many hairstyles that I'm sure that when we finally leave the compound and go to the United States of America, Lucinda will be bald.

"Lucinda, *por favor*, pretty please, tell me what is going on?" I promise her a back rub that she doesn't have to pay me for.

Lucinda puts her hairbrush down on her vanity and makes a sign for me to follow her to the patio out back.

"We should be okay out here," she whispers, looking over her shoulder.

"Why are you whispering?" In fact, everyone has been talking in whispers and low voices this last week, as if the house is full of fussy babies who've finally fallen asleep.

Lucinda explains. The SIM have probably hidden microphones in the house and are monitoring our conversations from their VWs.

"Why are they treating us like criminals? We haven't done anything wrong."

"Shhh!" Lucinda hushes me. For a moment she looks doubtful about continuing to explain things to a little sister who can't keep her voice down. "It's all about T-O-N-I," she says, spelling out our uncle's name in English. "A few months ago, he and his friends were involved in a plot to get rid of our dictator."

"You mean. . . ." I don't even have to say our leader's name. Lucinda nods solemnly and puts a finger to her lips.

Now I'm *really* confused. I thought we liked El Jefe. His picture hangs in our front entryway with the saying below it: IN THIS

HOUSE, TRUJILLO RULES. "But if he's so bad, why does Mrs. Brown hang his picture in our classroom next to George Washington?"

"We have to do that. Everyone has to. He's a dictator."

I'm not really sure what a dictator does. But this is probably not a good time to ask.

It turns out that the SIM discovered the plot and most of our uncle's friends were arrested. As for Tío Toni, nobody knows where he is. "He might be hiding out or they"—Lucinda looks over her shoulder. I know just who she means—"they might have him in custody."

"Will they disappear him?"

Lucinda seems surprised that I know about such matters. "Let's hope not," she sighs. Tío Toni is a special favorite of hers. At twenty-four, he's not that much older than she, at fifteen, and he is very handsome. All her girlfriends have crushes on him. "Ever since the SIM uncovered that plot, they've been after the family. That's why everyone's left. Tío Carlos and Mamita and Papito—"

"Why don't we leave, too, since we're not going to school anyway?"

"And abandon Tío Toni?" Lucinda shakes her head vigorously. Her pretty auburn hair is up in this hairdo called a chignon, like Princess Grace wears in her magazine wedding pictures. It comes undone and cascades down her back. "What if he comes back? What if he needs our help?" Her voice has risen above her usual whispering.

For once in the last few weeks, it's my turn to tell someone else in our house, "SHHHH!"

About two weeks after my cousins leave, Mr. Washburn comes for a visit. He has been stopping by briefly every day since the SIM raid. "How're those little ole bugs?" he asks mysteriously, looking out the window to where the black Volkswagens are still parked. Papi always replies, "Still biting."

But this evening, Mr. Washburn has a proposition to make. He sits in the study with Papi, talking in English. Mami looks from one to the other as if she's at a tennis match eagerly awaiting the outcome of the game. Unlike Papi, Mami has a hard time with English.

"Sounds like a great idea," my father is saying. "Anita!" He calls me in from the hallway, where I've been trying to be invisible so no one will ask me to leave. "We're going to have neighbors. What do you think of that?"

Just as long as the neighbors aren't the SIM, I'll be glad for anyone living in the compound with us. It's creepy being in a place with so many empty houses. Besides, I'm so lonely and bored without Carla or any of my other cousins around. "Who's moving in?" I ask.

"*El señor* Washburn," my mother says, smiling. It's the happiest I've seen her in weeks. With someone from the United States embassy living next door, the SIM might not bother us anymore.

But the best news of the evening is that Mr. Washburn has a family that will be joining him—a wife and two kids!

"How old are they?" I interrupt.

"*Cotorrita*," Mami reminds me.

"Sammy's twelve and Susie will be fifteen in February."

"I'm going to be twelve next week!" I blurt out in English. Mami hushes my rudeness again, but I can tell she is proud of my being confident in a language she finds so hard to learn.

Mr. Washburn gives me a wide smile. "Happy birthday in advance. And by the way, young lady, you speak English very well."

That night, I replay his compliment over and over in my head. It's the nicest thing that has happened to me in weeks. Actually, the second nicest, because a few days later, the Washburns move in. And the SIM move out!

I watch through the hibiscus hedge as workmen carry boxes into the Garcías' house. A boy follows them, his hair so blond it looks almost white, as if it sat in a bucket of bleach overnight. Later, after everything has been taken inside, the workmen come out and set up a trampoline under the tall ceiba tree. Then the boy climbs up on it. I'm sure he's going to tear a hole in that trampoline the way he jumps and jumps on it.

One time when he's up in the air, he catches sight of me lurking behind the hedge. "Howdy Doody!" he hollers. At first, I think he's calling me dirty, "Howdy, Dirty!" Before I can think what to do, he jumps off the trampoline and comes over.

"It's Howdy Doody time! It's Howdy Doody time!" he sings as he pumps my hand. I must look very confused because he asks me if I've ever watched Howdy Doody on TV. He talks so fast in English that I'm not sure I understand what he's saying.

"We don't have a TV," I explain.

"You *don't?*" He looks surprised. "But I thought you were rich. My dad says you own this whole park!"

"It's not a park," I correct. "It's a compound."

"What's that mean?" His blue eyes light up. "Is it like a harem?"

I'm not sure what a harem is, so I know the compound can't be that. I explain how my grandparents bought the land way back, and when each of their kids got married, they built a house on the property, and that's how the place became the family compound, which really is just five houses and one bachelor pad, surrounded by a high wall to keep strangers out, and lots of us grandkid-cousins dressed in each other's hand-me-downs. "But now everybody but us left for the United States of America," I say sadly.

"That's where I'm from," Sammy says, puffing out his chest, as if someone is going to pin a medal on it. "Greatest country in the world."

I want to contradict him and say that my own country is the greatest. But I'm not sure anymore after what Lucinda told me about us having a dictator who makes everybody hang his picture on their walls.

"Want me to teach you the property?" I offer, eager to change the subject. When he stares back blankly, I know I haven't said what I want to say in English.

"You mean, do I want you to show it to me?"

I hang my head with embarrassment.

"No big deal," he adds. "I never do good in English and it's my native language."

I like him instantly for not making fun of my English.

"Let me tell my mom," he says before we set off. When he comes running back out, a tall, red-headed woman wearing a frilly apron stands at the door waving hello to me.

We spend the rest of the afternoon exploring the compound—the lily pond with wishing coins we can't see at the bottom because it's gotten so slimy; the old Taino cemetery, where Mundín discovered a carved stone Chucha said would bring rain; the wild, overgrown plot where my maiden aunt Mimí will someday build a house if she ever gets married. Showing it off to somebody makes the place I've always known suddenly a lot more interesting. But I can't show him everything because a little later, his mom calls him inside to get his room in order so he can sleep in it tonight.

"See you later, alligator," Sammy yells over his shoulder.

"Tomorrow?" I ask.

"Sure," he calls back.

Just thinking about tomorrow's meeting, I feel so excited. I only wish Sammy had not called me an alligator. I know it's just a stupid American saying, but I really don't appreciate being called such an ugly animal. Even *cotorrita* is starting to get on my nerves. Honestly! People are always reminding me about my manners, but where are theirs?

The next day, Sam and I are exploring down by Tía Mimí's orchid shed, where the orchids have grown straggly since Porfirio left. Right next to the shed is the bachelor pad that Tío Toni built last year, a tiny *casita* like the ones in the country, with wooden shutters that latch up from the inside and a big padlock at the door. Tío Toni and his friends liked to sit around half the night talking in hushed voices. Now that I know what they were really up to, it feels creepy going near the place.

As we come in view of the *casita*, I stop in my tracks as if I've seen a ghost. The door to Tío Toni's *casita* is opened a crack!

"What's up?" Sammy wants to know.

"It's not supposed to be open," I whisper. The *casita* has been shut up since late summer, when Tío Toni disappeared.

"Maybe your maid left it that way when she cleaned?" Sammy suggests. By now he looks a little nervous himself and is talking in whispers.

I shake my head. Chucha is the only one left working in the compound. She doesn't have time to do extra cleaning.

Slowly, we creep up to the door and glance in. Someone is moving around in the darkness inside!

We run back so fast that I can feel my heart racing long after my legs have stopped. Later, bouncing together on Sammy's trampoline, we promise not to tell our parents about our discovery just yet or they won't let us explore the compound anymore. We jump up and down, trying to touch the lowest branches on the ceiba tree. When Mrs. Washburn comes out with lemonade, we climb off the trampoline.

"How are you children doing?" she asks. She has big, blue, wide-open eyes and looks as if she is always surprised.

"Fine and dandy," Sam says quickly, raising a finger when his mother isn't looking and crossing his lips.

three

Secret Santas

Now that the SIM are gone and the Washburns are living next door, Mami and Papi decide we can go back to school.

But first, Mami sits us down. "I don't want you talking about what happened with your friends," she warns.

"Why not?" I want to know.

Mami quotes one of Chucha's sayings, " 'No flies fly into a closed mouth.' " The less said, the better. "And that includes talking to Susie and Sammy," Mami adds, eyeing Lucinda and me.

Lucinda has become friends with Sammy's older sister, just as I have with Sammy. Poor Mundín is stuck without a new friend. But he says he doesn't care. Papi is giving him extra responsibility, taking him to work the days we aren't in school. Some nights after supper, Mundín gets to drive the car up and down all the driveways that connect the houses in the compound.

"If anything happens to me," Papi says from time to time, "you're the man of the house."

"If he wants to be the man of the house, he's going to have to stop biting his nails," Mami says, breaking the tense silence that follows such remarks.

The night before going back to school, I spend a long time picking out my outfit, as if I'm getting ready for the first day of classes. Finally, I settle on the parrot skirt Mami made me in imitation of the poodle skirt all the American girls are wearing. But even after everything is laid out, I feel apprehensive about going back. Everyone will be asking me why I've been absent for over two weeks. I myself don't understand why we weren't able to go to school just because the SIM were on our doorstep. After all, Papi still went to work every day. But Mami has refused to even discuss it.

I go next door to Lucinda's room. My sister is setting her hair in rollers. Talk about torture! How can she sleep with those rods in her hair? For her outfit, she also picked out her skirt just like my parrot skirt, but she insisted on a poodle when Mami made hers.

"*Linda* Lucinda," I butter her up. "What are we going to tell everyone at school? You know they're going to be asking us where we were."

Lucinda sighs and rolls her eyes at herself in the mirror. She motions for me to come closer. "Don't talk in here," she whispers.

"Why?" I say out loud.

She gives me a disgusted look.

"Why?" I whisper in her ear.

"Very funny," she says.

I sit around until she's done with her rollers. Then she jerks her head for me to go out on the patio, where we can talk.

"If people ask, just tell them we had the chicken pox," Lucinda says.

"But we didn't."

Lucinda closes her eyes until she regains her patience with me. "I know we didn't have the chicken pox, Anita. It's just a story, okay?"

I nod. "But why didn't we really go to school?"

Lucinda explains that after our cousins' departure, too many upsetting things have been happening and that's why Mami hasn't wanted us out of her sight. Raids by the SIM, like the one we had; arrests; accidents.

"I heard Papi talking about some accident with butterflies or something," I tell her.

"*The* Butterflies," Lucinda corrects me, nodding. "They were friends of Papi. He's really upset. Everyone is. Even the Americans are protesting."

"Protesting what? Wasn't it a car accident?"

Lucinda's rolls her eyes again at how little I know. " 'Car accident,' " she says, making quote marks in the air with her fingers, as if she doesn't really mean what she's saying.

"You mean, they were—"

"Shhh!" Lucinda hushes me.

Suddenly, I understand. These women were murdered in a pretend accident! I shiver, imagining myself on the way to school, tumbling down a cliff, my parrot skirt flying up around me. Now I feel scared of leaving the compound. "So why send us to school at all?"

"The Americans are our friends," Lucinda reminds me. "So for now, we're safe."

I don't like the sound of "for now," or how Lucinda makes those quote marks in the air again when she says "we're safe."

Mami is actually a lot calmer now that the Washburns have moved in. Not only is it nice to have the special protection of the consul next door, but the extra rent money is coming in handy. Construcciones de la Torre isn't doing well. Everything is at a standstill because of the embargo, whatever that is. We're having to cut corners and sell off our uncles' cars and the furniture from my grandparents' house from when Papito was making money. I offer to let

Mami sell my brown oxfords and old-fashioned jumpers I don't like. But she smiles and says that won't be necessary just yet.

Lucinda and I aren't the only ones to make friends with our neighbors. Mami starts a canasta group to introduce Mrs. Washburn to other Dominican ladies and help her practice her Spanish. Two or three tables are set up on the back patio. The ladies chat in lowered voices. Every once in a while, the new maid, Lorena, comes around with a tray of lemonades or clean ashtrays. Although Mami is trying to save money, there's too much work keeping up with all the houses in the compound for just Chucha. So Mami has hired the young girl to help out. But we have to be extra careful what we say around her.

"Why?" I ask. "Because she's new?"

Mami gives me a look that has "*Cotorrita!*" written all over it. After I told Mami that her nickname for me was really getting on my nerves, she promised to stop using it. But she still lets me know with her eyes when I'm speaking up too much. "Just be careful what you say," Mami repeats.

I guess you can't trust a maid who hasn't changed anyone's diaper in the family!

Actually, I can't really complain about being asked to keep secrets. Sammy and I haven't said a word about our discovery. Twice we've gone back to Tío Toni's *casita* only to find the door closed and the padlock in place. But there have been fresh footprints leading to and from the *casita* and a pile of cigarette butts, as if someone without an ashtray has thrown them out the window.

"Very fishy," Sammy observes, an expression which he says means that something strange is going on.

Our compound is crawling with fish, all right.

* * *

At school, any interest in my disappearance for two weeks is upstaged by two much more exciting developments: Christmas is coming *and* Sammy has joined our class.

"Samuel Adams Washburn," Mrs. Brown introduces him.

"Sam," Sammy corrects her.

Mrs. Brown asks "Samuel" to come to the front of the room and say a little something about himself. Mostly, Sam shrugs as Mrs. Brown introduces him herself.

Then Mrs. Brown goes down each row, and we have to introduce ourselves. When my turn comes, Sam pipes up, "I know Anita already." My face burns with pleasure.

Behind me, Nancy Weaver and Amy Cartwright giggle their flirty hellos. I feel a pang of jealousy! Being Americans, they'll have so much more to share with Sam than I do.

I knew him first! I want to shout. *He's living in my cousins' house next door!*

Not that I think of Sam as a boyfriend, which I'm not allowed to have anyway. Mami doesn't approve of my being around any boys who aren't related to me. But since my cousins moved away, the rules have both tightened and loosened in odd ways. I can't talk about the SIM's visit or my cousins' leaving for New York City, but I can have Sam for a best friend even if he is a boy.

After we all introduce ourselves, Mrs. Brown says she has an announcement to make. "Class, we are going to play a special game for Christmas!" Everyone cheers. Mrs. Brown holds a finger to her lips to hush us. When we quiet down, she continues. "You will each pick a name out of a hat, and you'll be that classmate's Secret Santa—"

Oscar's hand is in the air before Mrs. Brown is done explaining, which is something we're not supposed to do.

Mrs. Brown ignores him. "As a Secret Santa, you'll be leaving hidden notes for the person whose name you've picked. Little gifts and surprises. Things like that. Then, at our Christmas party, you'll each find out who your Secret Santa has been." Mrs. Brown claps her hands at the fun this is going to be.

"Any questions?" Mrs. Brown adds, looking over at Oscar, who waves his hand eagerly. The class groans.

"What if you pick your own name?" Oscar wants to know.

Mrs. Brown thinks for a moment. "That is a good question. I suppose the best thing would be to put the name back in the hat and try again."

I look over at Oscar. Sometimes he is sort of smart. He's about Sammy's height but with a permanent suntan, as the American kids sometimes describe our color of skin. Oscar is actually only half Dominican, on his mother's side. His father, who's originally from Italy, works at the Italian embassy, which is why Carla and I have always thought Mrs. Brown is more patient with Oscar than with the rest of us "natives."

It sounds like this Secret Santa game could be fun, although now that Carla is gone, there's only one other person whose Secret Santa I want to be. I lift my chain out from inside my blouse and put the little cross in my mouth. Somehow it makes me feel closer to God. "*Por favor*, please, please, let it be Sammy," I plead.

But when I unfold my piece of paper, the name on it is Oscar Mancini! I consider folding the paper back up and pretending I picked my own name. But it seems like a mean thing to do, especially at Christmas.

The Secret Santa idea is short-lived. The next day in class, Mrs. Brown announces that due to some parental complaints, she is going to have to cancel the game. The class groans. "I know, class," Mrs. Brown says, pulling herself up as if someone has hurt her feelings, but she can't say who. "I'm disappointed, too."

At recess, we all find out from Amy and Nancy what has happened. Some Dominican parents complained to the principal about having Secret Santas.

I'm not surprised the complaints have come from Dominican parents, many of whom don't like the idea of Santa Claus's replacing the three wise kings. But it turns out that the objections aren't religious. Instead, some parents feel that there's enough tension in the air. Kids sneaking around and leaving secret messages might be taken the wrong way.

"Oh, come on!" Amy says, rolling her eyes. "What are they talking about?"

"It's the embargo," Oscar explains. Everyone looks over at him. None of us are really sure what an embargo is.

"Many countries will not have anything to do with us anymore," Oscar continues. "Including the United Estates," he adds, nodding at Amy as if she ordered the embargo herself.

"That's ridiculous," Nancy says. "If we didn't want anything to do with you, why would we be here?" She rolls her eyes at Amy, who rolls her eyes back at her.

Oscar considers this for a moment. "I don't know," he finally admits. "But my parents are preoccupied and that is why they do not wish anything sneaky to go on."

"So, it was *your* parents who complained!" Nancy says, hooking her arm into Amy's. The two girls stalk off toward where Sammy is bouncing a basketball with some of his new friends.

"Secret Santas are not sneaky!" Amy calls over her shoulder.

Whatever Secret Santas are or are not, I sincerely hope that my parents aren't among the complainers. But at supper that night, when I mention that the Secret Santa game has been canceled, the relieved look on their faces makes me suspect they also spoke to the principal.

"There are enough secrets"—Mami stops while Lorena brings in the flan dessert and clears the dinner plates—"enough secrets in the world already," Mami says as if she herself isn't always asking us to add to that amount!

In class, Mrs. Brown tries explaining how an embargo works. Sometimes a group of countries disapproves of what another country is doing, and they refuse to trade or do business with that country until the situation improves.

"As you know," Mrs. Brown is saying, "the United States has now joined the embargo."

Oscar turns and gives Nancy and Amy an I-told-you-so nod.

A dozen hands go up. Lots of the American students have questions. Is it okay for them to be in a country that is being embargoed? Are they behind enemy lines? Will they be taken prisoner?

Mrs. Brown shakes her head and laughs. "Heavens, no!" she reassures them. "It's not like that at all. Countries can disagree but life goes on. The United States wants to be friends with this country. How many of you have a teenage brother or sister?"

Lots of hands go up.

"You know how your parents will sometimes ground your brother or sister? It's not because they don't love him or her, now, is it? It's because they're concerned and want to make him or her a better person."

The more I think about it, an embargo sounds an awful lot like the punishment chair at home whenever we misbehave.

"So how has the Dominican Republic misbehaved?" one of the Dominican students wants to know.

But that is a question Mrs. Brown won't answer. "Enough about politics, class! We have our own politics to take care of. We're going to have to have an election today."

It turns out that Joey Farland, our current president, will be leaving over Christmas vacation. His dad, Ambassador Farland, has been recalled to Washington, D.C., because of the embargo. Sam's dad, Mr. Washburn, is in charge of the embassy that's now only a consulate. Something like that.

When Mrs. Brown asks for nominations, Nancy raises her hand. "Sam Washburn," she announces. The whole class breaks out clapping, as if Sammy has already won.

At school, I'm too shy to fight my way into the inner circle of Sam's fans. But back at the compound, we're still good pals. I draw him a map of the whole place and tell him some of the stories Tío Toni has told me about Sir Francis Drake and his pirates burying treasure on the property when they raided the island back in the 1500s, or about the Taino Indians having once had a burial yard behind Tío Fran's house that is full of spirits now—stories that are exciting to tell even if I don't really believe them anymore.

"Wow!" Sam keeps saying. "Pirates and ghosts right here where we're standing?"

I nod. I just love impressing the most popular boy in our class! We might not have the greatest country on earth, but we certainly have an interesting one!

One afternoon, while Chucha and Mami are out shopping, we sneak into Chucha's room and I show Sammy her coffin.

"Wow!" he says, glancing around at Chucha's purple towel

hanging from a peg, her purple mosquito net strung between two nails, her purple dresses draped over a chair. "Does everything she wear have to be purple?"

I nod. "Even her panties and stuff have to be dyed." My face burns as I realize I'm talking about underwear to a boy.

But Sammy is too busy peering into the coffin to notice. "Why's the inside all ripped up?"

I'm about to tell him how the SIM overturned the coffin and stuck their knives in the lining. But then I remember Mami's orders not to discuss the SIM raid with anyone.

"You know what I bet happened?" Sammy guesses. "I bet the lid came down one night and she had to claw her way out." Sammy makes claws with his fingers. His face has gotten flushed, as it always does when he gets excited. "Don't you think that's what happened?"

I don't know what's worse, telling a secret or a lie. So I shrug to be on the safe side. No flies fly into a closed mouth, I remind myself.

I suppose Mami is right to say that there are enough secrets in the world already. I could make a long list just of the secrets in our compound: my cousins' sudden departure, the SIM's two-week stay in our driveway, the intruder in Tío Toni's *casita*, the fresh footprints, the cigarette butts by the porch. One day, I bump into Chucha hurrying toward the back of the property, carrying food tins stacked in a carrier. "Where are you going, Chucha?" I ask.

"Mi secreto, tu silencio," she whispers—one of her old sayings, "My secret, your silence"—and hurries away.

Sometimes, the phone rings, and when I answer, whoever's at the other end hangs up.

But one time, a man's voice asks for Don Mundo, and after I call Papi in his study, I stay at my end to make sure he picks up before I set the receiver down. "Don Mundo?" the voice asks. "*¿Cómo están las cosas?*" How are things?

"We're waiting for Mr. Smith's tennis shoes," Papi says. It is such an odd reply that, though I had meant to hang up, I stay on.

"They'll be at Wimpy's," the voice replies, and hangs up.

Wimpy's? Wimpy's is the fancy grocery store where mostly Americans and other foreigners shop. The doors are made of glass and open magically as you approach. The air-conditioning is cranked so high, you have to bring a sweater along. Chucha claims the place is bewitched, and she refuses to go inside whenever Mami goes shopping there.

Slowly, I place the receiver back in its cradle.

My parents seem to be playing their own kind of Secret Santa game.

School is out for the holidays. This is usually my favorite vacation—first my birthday and then Christmas. But with everyone gone, I'm not looking forward to the loneliness. Thank goodness the Washburns have moved in next door.

On my birthday, Mami offers to invite Sam over, but I already told him I was twelve two weeks ago, so I don't want to be caught in a lie. My birthday cake is in the shape of a heart this year. Mami is known for her fancy cakes, but she can't get good flour or the American food dye, so she uses a *criollo* brand that turns the cake a purply color instead of the rose red she wanted. Chucha, of course, is delighted.

Because of the embargo, some of the American foods we usually eat at Christmas are not available or are too expensive. This year, there will be no red apples in a bowl or candy canes on a little dish to offer visitors. Mr. Nutcracker won't have walnuts, only almonds from the almond tree behind Mamita and Papito's house.

Also, I'll only be getting one gift this year. I try to decide between a charm for my bracelet or a diary with a little lock and key like Lucinda got last Christmas. I finally settle on the diary because Mami hints that gold is too expensive right now on our budget. But truly, what I want most of all is to have my family back together again.

"We're still going to have a lovely time," Mami promises.

The Saturday before Christmas, we go shopping in the open air *mercado* for roasted pig, avocados, guava paste, and ripe plantains for *plátanos maduros*, the different merchants calling out their wares from their stands. Beside them on the ground sits a pile of their little children, in rags, looking up at me. I feel both lucky and ashamed.

Papi always says that we need a government that will give these children a chance, like the one the United States has. "Education is the key! Who knows if one of those little *tigueritos* in the *mercado* isn't an Einstein or Michelangelo or maybe even a Cervantes!" Mami hushes him with her usual "No flies fly into a closed mouth, Mundo." But her face is fierce with pride, as if Papi is a hero for saying what he thinks.

Monsito, the boy who helps us carry our sacks, always takes us to the best stands, where everything is fresh. He's about my size, but we don't really know how old he is. When Mami asks him, he just shakes his head and grins. "Don't you know when your birthday is?" I persist. He looks worried, as if he thinks he might get in trouble for not knowing. "Sixteen," he finally says, but it sounds like a guess. Mami says Monsito could very well be that old and still be as small as I am. "Poor kids who don't get good nutrition just don't grow."

Even though we are on a budget, Mami gives Monsito a big tip for his family to buy food for Christmas. She also gives him several pairs of Mundín's old trousers that probably won't fit Monsito until he's eighteen, or maybe never.

On the way back from the *mercado*, we drive slowly to look at all the sights. The roads are crowded. It seems as though everyone has come to the capital to see the decorations at the palace. A life-sized Nativity scene has been set up on the lawn below the towering statue of El Jefe on his horse. It looks as if those shepherds and camels and even Mary and Joseph have come all the way from Bethlehem just to see him.

We make a quick stop at Wimpy's to pick up one apple to put in the mouth of the roasted pig and a few dates for the delicious bread pudding, *pudín de pan*, we always eat on Christmas Day. "Luxuries for *Nochebuena*," Mami explains. I keep my eyes open for tennis shoes, but there don't seem to be any for sale.

Papi disappears to the back office with the owner, whose nickname, Wimpy, is also the name of his store. He's a former marine who came to the country with an occupation force years back, but once the troops left, he stayed on, marrying a rich Dominican lady and opening his successful grocery store. He has bulgy muscles with a tattooed eagle on his right arm. Sometimes he'll flex for us kids, and the eagle looks like it's flapping its wings.

When we're ready to leave the store, Papi is not with us. It turns out he's already outside in the parking lot, standing by the trunk of our car, one foot on the fender, smoking a cigarette and talking to Wimpy in a low, serious voice. In the backseat sits Chucha, arms crossed, glaring at the storefront. All I can think of is what Mami sometimes says to Lucinda when my older sister makes a face: "If looks could kill . . ."

We begin decorating the house to welcome the baby Jesus. One Sunday, we drive out to the beach and cut down a small sea grape tree, paint it white, and hang it with our lights that look like nose droppers filled with colored water. We place the olivewood crèche from Bethlehem, which was blessed by the Pope, under the tree and hang the lighted-up Santa face on the wall beside the portrait of El Jefe by the front door. Sometimes Papi pauses as he walks by, the reddish light illuminating his tense face. But it isn't Santa he's staring at with a fierce, if-looks-could-kill look in his eyes.

The night of *Nochebuena*, Mami and Papi throw a small "rooster" party, which will last till the wee hours when the cocks start to crow. They invite a few friends over, including the Washburns and Oscar's parents, the Mancinis. Oscar's mother, Doña Marina, has recently joined the canasta group, and during one of the games, Mami and she have discovered that they are related. They use the back of the score pad to sketch a whole forest of family trees. It's such a distant connection that I hope Oscar won't bring up our being kissing cousins at school.

Before everyone arrives, there's a special call from *Nueva York*. This time it isn't just Mamita and Papito or one of the uncles on the other end. Everyone is gathered together at my grandparents', and one by one we take the phone and shout, *"Feliz Navidad,"* as if it were volume and not the cable at the bottom of the sea that carried our voices over the miles. When my turn comes, Mami reminds me to mind what I say, but she doesn't have to worry. I'm so tongue-tied that I can't think of any of the dozen things I've saved up to tell Carla. "Did you get my card?" she shouts.

"No, not yet!" I shout back. All mail has to go through the censors first, so, especially at Christmas, it takes a long time to get a letter.

I stay up late, helping Lorena and Chucha pass around trays of the traditional rum punch. This year the glasses are smaller, but everyone is happy to be together. Papi lifts his glass and offers a toast. "May the new year bring peace and liberty. . . ." I can see Mami tense up, watching Lorena from the corner of her eye. Papi must sense some danger as well because he adds, "*Paz y libertad* to all the peoples of the world!"

"What do you want Santa Claus to bring you?" Mrs. Washburn asks me. I have to bite my tongue not to be fresh. It's true that I'm small for twelve, but I'm wearing Lucinda's hand-me-down patent leathers with the little heels that bring me up to almost five feet. Mami has also put some of her lipstick and rouge on me and sprayed hair spray in my hair to make me feel more grown-up. But I guess I still look like I'm twelve going on eleven.

Later, in bed, I keep waking to the dull, pleasant sound of voices coming from the patio outside my window. Toward midnight, everybody starts singing carols in English and Spanish, and sometimes in both languages combined, now the English overpowering the Spanish, and now the Spanish overpowering the English, depending on whose voices carry the tune of that song.

I finally fall asleep and dream that Santa has arrived in a black Volkswagen filled with cousins carrying baskets full of apples and raisins and nuts. He's knocking and knocking at our front door, but no one can hear him for all the party noise inside.

I sit bolt upright in bed, determined to let him in. An eerie silence fills the house. The guests seem to have left. I open the jalousies beside my bed and look out past the patio to the yard beyond. The party lanterns have been blown out and the garden is shrouded in darkness. But far off, at the back of the property, a light is shining in Tío Toni's *casita*, a glittering sparkle among the dark foliage. In my dazed and sleepy state, I feel a surge of joy, as if Secret Santa has arrived and I am a little kid again.

four

Disappeared Diary

Mrs. Brown always says that writing makes a person more thoughtful and interesting. I don't know about interesting, but the diary I got for Christmas is sure making me think about a lot of things.

Sam, for instance. His blond-white hair that no longer seems too white . . . his dreamy blue eyes, like a daydreamy sky . . . and suddenly, I'm thinking, I *do* want him as more than a friend, whether I'm allowed to have a boyfriend or not!

Before I wrote all this out, I really didn't know I felt this way deep down.

I always write with a pencil for a reason. I want to be sure that on a moment's notice, I can erase what I've written. I still have Carla's huge eraser. With a few strokes back and forth, I can get rid of any evidence if the SIM come to our door.

Another danger is Mami. Not that my mother is the nosy kind, as she believes God in heaven can see you and that is supervision enough. But given how nervous she is these days, and given the trouble we seem to be in, and supposing a diary should just happen to fall out from under a pillow as she's straightening a bed, her eyes might read a sentence like "I think I am falling in love with Samuel Adams Washburn," and that'll be the end of my being allowed to have Sam as any kind of a friend.

So whenever I write down something personal, I let it stay written for the rest of the day, like savoring a piece of hard candy before biting down on it. Then, at night, I erase that page to be on the safe side.

I haven't told Sam about my diary because I know he'll ask to see it. I do mention that my parents always review my letters to Carla before I send them off. As for Carla's letters to me, a messy censor must read them because the envelopes come torn and taped, with whole sentences sometimes blocked out.

Sam tells me about this invention in the United States called invisible ink that lets you write stuff down so that no one can read it until the page is soaked in a chemical that makes all the letters reappear.

I wish I had a bottle of that ink for writing in my diary because the truth is I feel kind of sad writing in pencil, always prepared to erase. But Sammy says that ink is probably not sold anywhere in the country, not even at Wimpy's.

School is supposed to reopen on Monday, January 9, soon after Epiphany, but we get a notice from the principal that classes will not resume until the end of the month. It turns out a lot of the Americans are traveling to Washington, D.C., for the inauguration of their new president, Mr. John F. Kennedy. Many, like the Farlands, won't be coming back.

Since Papi knows Mr. Farland from when he went to school in the States, we go over to say good-bye. Wimpy and Mr. Washburn are there, too. Papi joins them out on the patio. Little snatches of their conversation drift in: "tennis shoes," "outrage at the Butterflies," "CIA intervention . . ." Before I can puzzle out what they're saying, Mrs. Farland calls me away from the door. "Anita, sweetie, come over here and let Joey tell you about the inauguration for our new president."

I know all about how the Americans run their country because we have to study it at school. Every four years, they have a contest, and whoever wins gets to be the *jefe*. But he can't just keep being the *jefe*. He can only win the contest twice, and then he has to give somebody else a chance.

We have elections, too, but there's only one person in the contest, Trujillo, and he has already been our *jefe* for thirty-one years. I once asked Mrs. Brown why nobody ran against him, and she hesitated and said that perhaps it would be better if I asked my parents that question. When I asked Mami, she said, "Ask your father," and when I asked Papi, he told me to go ask Mami. After a while, I got tired of asking.

I can tell both Mami and Papi are really glad that Mr. Kennedy is going to be the American president. Mami thinks he is *muy guapo*, so handsome, with his hair in his eyes and *only* (?!) forty-three years old. He's also a Catholic, which is kind of like being related to us since we are in the same religious family. And most importantly, Papi says, Mr. Kennedy has declared himself a champion of democracy around the world.

At the next canasta gathering, Mami's friends all count off the families they know that have left the country. Mrs. Washburn confesses that Mr. Washburn has talked of sending his family away. She always calls her husband Mr. Washburn, as if no one will know whom she's talking about if she calls him plain Henry.

"I told Mr. Washburn, over my dead body," she announces to the table. "We leave when he leaves! We've got diplomatic immunity. That S.O.B.'s a dead duck if he dares lay a hand on us!"

None of the Dominican women say a word. They sip their *cafecitos* quietly and look at each other. Mami, whose English has improved tremendously since the arrival of the Washburns next door, says, "Doris, put the lid on the sugar bowl, *por favor*. There are so many flies."

I look around for flies, but there are none I can see. Lorena has just come out from the kitchen with a tray to collect the empty coffee cups. Perhaps she scared them away.

Then, just like that, it dawns on me: My mother is speaking to Mrs. Washburn in code. She's saying: *We are being overheard; be quiet.* It's as if I've stepped into a room I'm not supposed to be in— but now that I'm inside, the door has disappeared. I feel the same way as when Lucinda told me how one day I, too, would get my period. "What if I don't want to?" I asked, disgusted at the thought of bleeding between my legs. "You don't have a choice," she shot back.

Later, I write in my diary about the Washburn family maybe moving back to the United States. Just thinking about losing Sammy, I start to cry. Wiping my tears from the page, I smudge the writing so badly, I won't have to erase a thing tonight.

According to Mami, I'm developing the same case of bathroom-itis as Lucinda.

I roll my eyes when she says so. Can't I at least have my own diseases?! I'm told I have my mother's *café con leche* skin color, my father's curly black hair, my grandmother's slightly turned-up nose, the dimples from some great-aunt who spent her whole life smiling at everyone. I feel like just a hand-me-down human being!

Mami is right, of course. I *am* spending a lot more time in the bathroom. But I'm not about to tell her that it has nothing to do with my copying Lucinda and a lot to do with my liking Sam.

Liking a guy sure makes a girl think about whether she's pretty enough. I stand in front of the mirror, staring at myself. My black hair is a tangle of curls. My nose is average. My mouth is average. Come to think of it, my whole face is really pretty average. But Mrs. Washburn says I look a little like Audrey Hepburn with a suntan. When I tell Lucinda, all she says is "Dream on."

Still, if Mrs. Washburn thinks so, maybe Sam thinks so, too? I search Lucinda's old *Novedades* magazines and Mrs. Washburn's cast-off copies of *Look* and *Life* for pictures of Audrey Hepburn. But every one I find, I have to agree with Lucinda, and dream on.

One canasta afternoon, Mrs. Mancini brings Oscar along. Mami has told her that I would be *encantada*—enchanted!—to have my classmate around. When she says so, I have to do everything in my power not to roll my eyes. Mami says this is a terrible habit I've picked up since I turned twelve. (She must not have been looking at me when I was eleven!)

I'm worried that Sammy will not want to hang out with me if "cousin" Oscar is around. I stay in my room after Mami calls that my guests have arrived. When I finally come out to greet them, Oscar and Sammy have disappeared. I find them jumping on the trampoline, daring each other to see who can touch the branches of the ceiba tree.

Even though I've been worried that they'll be enemies, now I'm upset they've become friends without me. Sometimes, it's totally confusing to be me! Only writing in my diary helps me feel a little less crazy.

Oscar is the first to notice me. "*Hola*, Anita!"

Instead of waving back, I turn to go.

"What's wrong with her?" I hear Sammy ask.

"I think her feelings are hurt," Oscar replies. "Hey, Anita, wait up," he calls. I can't believe it's Oscar who understands my feelings, not Sammy, whom I'm secretly planning to marry.

When they catch up with me, it's also Oscar who says, "I was wondering where you were."

"Yeah," Sammy adds, and sunshine breaks upon my heart again.

"The entire country is in trouble," Oscar explains. We're sitting under the trampoline after having busted one of the ropes by all three jumping on it at once. "Mami saw Mrs. Brown at Wimpy's and she said the school might have to close because so many families are leaving."

"We're staying!" Sam announces proudly. "We've got amnesia."

"Amnesty," Oscar corrects. I bite my lip so as not to smile. Even though I'm almost in love with Sam Washburn, I can't resist feeling proud when a Dominican corrects an American's English. "But you mean immunity," Oscar goes on. "We have immunity, too, because my father is with the Italian embassy. Lots of people hide in the embassy because the SIM can't touch them if they're on another country's property. Like your uncle," he says, turning to me.

"Which uncle?" I want to know. Of course, I'm thinking of Tío Toni.

"I'm not supposed to mention names. But the embargo means countries are closing their embassies. That's why you don't have an embassy anymore," he points out to Sammy. "Just a consulate."

"My father's the consul," Sammy boasts.

"I know, but he's not the ambassador."

"So?"

Oscar shrugs. "Just that he can't help the people who want to free this country."

We are *free!* I want to cry out. But thinking about how the SIM raided our property, how Tío Toni had to disappear, how I have to erase everything in my diary, I know that Oscar is telling the truth. We're *not* free—we're trapped—the Garcías got away just in time! I feel the same panic as when the SIM came storming through our house.

"Your father," he points to Sammy, "and yours and mine, too," he adds, pointing to me and then to himself. "They all know about this, but they don't want to worry us."

"So, how do you know all of this stuff?" Sammy confronts him.

A slow grin spread across Oscar's face. "I ask a lot of questions."

So do I, I'm thinking, but until now I never got any answers.

All these things that Oscar tells us I write down in my diary.

I don't know what I'd do without it. It's like my whole world is coming undone, but when I write, my pencil is a needle and thread, and I'm stitching the scraps back together. Sometimes, I wake up in the middle of the night crying out. I cross the hall to Lucinda's room and slip in beside her. She seems to welcome my presence because she lets me stay there instead of telling me to scram, like in the old days.

The worst stories Oscar tells are the ones about El Jefe. When I first heard how bad he was from Lucinda, I felt so confused. Everyone had always treated El Jefe like God. I shudder to think how many times I've prayed to him instead of to Jesus on His cross.

"He does even worse things than crucify people," Oscar tells us one time. "He disappears them."

I remember Chucha saying the SIM disappeared people. "What exactly does that mean?" I ask Oscar. He's so much easier to talk to than Lucinda. I usually have to beg her and then throw in a free back rub before she'll tell me anything.

"He arrests people, then cuts out their eyes and fingernails, and throws their cadavers in the sea for the sharks to eat them."

"Wow!" Sammy says, impressed, his eyes greedy for more awful details.

I feel sick to my stomach. The thought of Tío Toni, eyeless and fingernail-less, is just too horrible to think about. But I don't want to throw up in front of a boy I'm falling in love with and a cousin I don't want to be related to. "We have a mystery ghost," I speak up, wanting to change the subject. I mean to make my news sound scary, but a ghost now seems harmless compared to what we just heard.

"He comes at night, then leaves during the day," Sam adds. I've told Sam about the light I saw at Tío Toni's house Christmas Eve. We fill Oscar in on all the particulars of the unlocked door and cigarette butts.

"Let's go see," Oscar insists.

As we head for the back of the property, we hear hurried foot-steps coming down the walk toward us.

"What are you doing back here?" Chucha questions, looking from one to the other, as if she's trying to figure out which one of us will be most likely to tell her the truth.

"We're allowed to," I announce, showing off in front of my friends.

Chucha levels her gaze at me. I know she's about to say that she's the one to allow or not to allow things, as she once changed my diapers.

Quickly, I back down and explain. "Somebody's been in Tío Toni's *casita*, Chucha."

Her dark eyes widen in warning. "You have to be very careful," she whispers, making the familiar gesture of cutting off her head. "Things will be happening soon for which there is no protection." She looks up at the sky and then all around her as if she sees signs everywhere. "No protection but silence, no protection but dark hiding places, wings, and prayers." Listening to her, I remember how Chucha sometimes sees the future in dreams. I shiver, wondering what she has seen.

Although Sam knows a little Spanish, he rarely understands Chucha, who has a tendency to mumble and mix in Haitian words with her Spanish. "What's she saying?" he wants to know.

"I'm not sure," I tell him. "Sometimes she talks in riddles and you have to try to figure out what she's saying." Turning back to my old nursemaid, I ask her what's uppermost on my mind. "Is Tío Toni all right?"

As if Chucha not only gives answers but makes them materialize, a face appears at the window of the small house. There's no mistaking the dark, curly hair, the strong jaw, the good looks that make pretty girls call up my aunt Mimí and ask if they can come over and look at her orchids. I feel a rush of relief to see my uncle intact, no eyes or fingernails missing. But I have sense enough not to call out his name.

"Who's that?" Sammy asks. He and Oscar are peering in the direction I'm looking.

I don't know how Chucha can guess what Sammy has asked, since she doesn't know a word of English, but she replies, "Tell the *americanito* that it's someone he did not see."

Even though I know English, I don't know how to translate something that makes no sense at all, even to me.

* * *

Tell him it's someone he did not see, I'm writing in my diary when there's a knock on the door. *"Un momentito, por favor,"* I call out, and quickly erase the page I've been writing before shoving the diary back under my pillow.

It's Mami at the door. "Everything all right?" she asks, looking around the room, probably wondering what I'm hiding that I need the delay of *"un momentito"* before I say, "Come in."

"I want to show you something," Mami says, motioning mysteriously for me to follow her outside.

She leads the way out past the patio and around the front of Mamita and Papito's house to the pond that used to be filled with Tía Mimí's water lilies. Now it's covered by a layer of green scum and overrun by bullfrogs. We sit on the stone bench, and Mami takes my hands in hers.

"I know many unusual things have been happening, Anita," she begins. "And I know there are many questions and worries in your head." She touches my face ever so gently, as if she wants to banish all the worries that have been piling up in the last month. "Suddenly, you have to be a big girl—"

"I *am* twelve, Mami!" I sigh and roll my eyes. Recently, if anyone talks to me as if I'm a little kid, I get mad. But I also feel sad that I'm not a little kid anymore and that I know as much as I do. I've written about these confused feelings in my diary, too, but this is one confusion that doesn't get any clearer by writing about it.

"You *are* a young lady," Mami agrees. "And I'm going to confide in you the way I do in Lucinda and your brother. Okay?" she adds uncertainly, as if she isn't sure whether to take the next step.

I roll my eyes. "Mami, I know a lot more stuff than you think I do!"

"Oh?"

I wonder if now is the time to tell her about all the scary things Oscar has told me or about seeing Tío Toni at the window of his *casita*. But I'm afraid if I say a word, Mami might never get to her story. "Just stuff about becoming a *señorita*."

Mami hesitates. "Have you gotten . . . your period?"

I shake my head. I used to think when I started bleeding between my legs, Mami would be the first to know. Now I'm not so sure that I want to tell Mami something that personal.

"What happened was your uncles and their friends were unhappy with the government and they had a plan that the SIM found out about." Mami's story follows the same lines as what Lucinda has told me. "Many of those friends were arrested. Some, like Tío Carlos, left the country. Some were killed."

Mami stops a moment and wipes her eyes. Then her hands curl up into fists on her lap.

"At first, your father didn't want to endanger his family. But sometimes life without freedom is no life at all."

It sounds scary. Like something someone facing a firing squad might say before they're shot. "Then why not go be free with the rest of the family in *Nueva York*?" I ask, hoping that she'll reassure me that we're not trapped, that we can leave if we want to.

"No!" Mami says, her hands formed into fists. "What would have happened to the United States if George Washington had left his country? Or if Abraham Lincoln had said, 'I've had enough'? The Negro people would still be slaves."

I feel ashamed of myself for being a scaredy-cat. I think about what Papi has said about having a country where everyone, including Monsito, can have a chance.

"And someday," Mami continues, "we will be free, and all your cousins and aunts and uncles will come back and thank us."

She looks around at the scraggly grounds, the overgrown bushes, the abandoned houses. A sad look crosses her face. "In fact, the embargo is already helping. Some observers are here from other countries and the government's trying to show off how fair it is. That means all Tío Toni's friends in prison have been freed. Things are going to change, but until that day, we have to be patient and make some sacrifices."

I knew she'd get to the hard part sooner or later.

"Your uncle Toni has been . . . in hiding," she explains, choosing her words carefully. "Now he can come out. But the SIM can still decide at any minute to take him away. He's pretty safe in the compound with Mr. Washburn next door. But it's best if you and Sammy and Oscar avoid going back there." She nods in the direction of the *casita*. "Also, you are not to speak about this to anyone. Only to your pillow . . ."

I must look guilty just thinking about what's hidden under my pillow right this very moment. It's as if my mother can read my thoughts. "One last big favor to ask you, *mi amor*. No more writing in your diary for the time being."

"That's so unfair!" Mami gave me the diary for Christmas. Telling me not to write in it is like taking away my only present.

"I know it is, Anita." Mami wipes away my tears with her thumbs. "For now, we have to be like the little worm in the cocoon of the butterfly. All closed up and secret until the day . . ." She spreads her arms as if they were wings.

Hearing the thrill in her voice, how can I refuse her anything she asks me?

I go back to my room and erase every page of my diary. Then I put it away in my closet beside Carla's things. Until the day.

five

Mr. Smith

Now that I'm grounded from roaming the property, I spend a lot of time playing card games with Sam on our patio. I really don't understand why Mami has to be so cautious. With the consul living next door, marines guard the compound round the clock. Sometimes, I wake to the *click-clop* of their boots as they patrol the grounds at night.

We play casino and canasta and concentration. Susie and Lucinda, who are as bored as we are, join us. Except for school, which has finally reopened, we don't go out anymore. Parents are being cautious, especially the parents of young ladies.

"Why's that?" I ask. We're sitting on the patio, playing casino.

Susie fans out her cards in her hand. Her nails are painted pale pink like the inside of a conch shell. "On account of Mr. Smith," she says, eyeing Lucinda meaningfully. Both girls burst into giggles when Sam and I ask together, "Who's Mr. Smith?"

"Mr. Smith's not his real name." Susie lowers her voice. Even she whispers when we get onto certain subjects. "He's a very powerful guy. And he likes girls—young, pretty girls. So parents won't let their daughters go out to public places where they might be seen by Mr. Smith. Because if he sees them and wants them, he gets what he wants."

I shudder and look over at Lucinda. The nervous rash on her neck has reddened, and she's scratching it.

"Hey, genius, who's winning?" Susie asks Sam, who is keeping score. She often addresses her younger brother with sarcasm. "Ooooh, Lucy-baby! You've got fifteen. Lucky number!"

In two weeks, Susie will be turning fifteen. Lucinda has told her how a girl's fifteenth birthday is really important in our country. Some parents throw *quinceañera* parties as lavish as weddings. "We just have to do something for your birthday," Lucinda insists.

"Like what? We can't go to the country club, we can't go to the beach." Susie goes through her list of grievances. I have a feeling that she goes through this list often with her mother, probably as often as Lucinda does with ours. "I'm *soooo* bored. I wouldn't mind a little excitement." Susie lets out a long sigh, just like her mother when she has a bad hand.

"How come you don't just have a party here?" Sam says absently. He's tallying up the scores again—and again he has the lowest score so far. "This place is like a country club."

Both girls look at him as if he has sprouted wings.

"Well, it is," he adds defensively.

"Samuel, dear," Susie says, "that's a *fantástico* idea!" She reaches over and smacks a kiss on her brother's cheek, which he immediately wipes off, making his I've-got-an-anaconda-around-my-neck face.

"My brother, the genius," Susie declares, this time without sarcasm.

At first, Susie's parents are not keen on a big *quinceañera* party. "They wanted me to wait until I'm sixteen!" she complains to Lucinda and me. We're practicing the twist in her room, listening to a guy called Chubby Checker on Susie's portable record player. Sammy's out at a Scouts' meeting, so I've been invited to join them. Lucinda usually tells me to scram when she's with one of her girlfriends. But recently, she's being a lot nicer to me. Maybe she's realizing I'm not just a stupid little sister but a potential friend. Well, *potential friend* is maybe stretching it!

" 'Now, Susan Elizabeth,' " Susie says, imitating her parents, " 'you can have a big party for your sweet sixteen back in the States.' Can you believe it?"

"That's terrible," Lucinda says.

I nod. "I didn't have a party for my birthday, either," I offer.

"Poor kid," Susie commiserates. "But guess what?" Her face is full of excitement. I know better than to take a guess.

"I told my parents what you guys told me about fifteen being the big birthday here. They're the ones always saying that in Rome you're supposed to do what the Romans do. Anyway, they said yes! So, we're going to twist, twist, twist all night." She raises the volume on Chubby Checker and we twist in celebration.

Susie's party is planned for her birthday, February 27, which is perfect, as that's our national independence day. "You'll have free fireworks," Lucinda notes.

For the next two weeks, it's as if someone is getting married in the compound. The Washburns hire two gardeners, who spiff up the grounds. The property begins to take on its old groomed look of a park. Paper lanterns are hung from tree to tree, and Tía Mimí's lily pond is cleaned out so we can again see the coins we once threw in for good luck. The canasta group meets daily to make party favors and help with the invitations. The party will start with refreshments, followed by dancing—rock and roll on the record player for Susie's friends and merengues and cha-chas by a live Dominican combo for her parents' guests. Susie's *quinceañera* has become a full-blown reception by the consul. But it can't be helped, Mr. Washburn explains. In the touchy atmosphere of a country under embargo, you have to be careful not to step on any toes.

In our own house, Lucinda tries on every one of her dressy dresses, Mami watching and commenting. They have an ongoing argument about necklines and bare shoulders. Finally, they settle on a strapless pale yellow gown, a hand-me-down from a glamorous aunt who used to be a beauty queen before she married and had kids. It has a narrow waist and a crinoline skirt that bells out like a ballerina's tutu. Lucinda agrees to wear a shawl, not to be modest, but to hide the rash on her neck that won't go away. "That shawl must not come off," Mami keeps reminding Lucinda, who is disgusted enough to roll her eyes at me in the absence of a friend her own age.

"As for you, young lady," Mami says, turning to me, "I hope you know this is an exception."

Of course, I know that going to a night party where there will be boys is unusual for a girl who has not yet turned fifteen. But this is supposed to be a "family gathering," hosted by our neighbors next door. I'm glad I haven't told Mami about my feelings for Sam, or she would make me stay home, trying to fall asleep to Elvis Presley howling "You Ain't Nothing but a Hound Dog," or the merengue band singing "Compadre Pedro Juan" and "Last Night I Dreamt About You."

(And I would die if I didn't get to dance with Sammy!)

Tío Toni is back. Every night, visitors drop in to see him. They sit on our patio, talking for hours. Sometimes, they walk off to his *casita* for more privacy. Mr. Washburn often joins them.

Papi and Tío Toni usually speak in English with Mr. Washburn. They both went to school in the States, Papi to Yale, which poor Mami always mispronounces *"jail."* The first time she met Mrs. Washburn, Mami bragged that her husband had gone to jail. The consul's wife smiled tensely and said, "Oh, dear, that's too bad," which baffled Mami completely, as she thought Yale was the school where the best families in the United States educated their sons.

Tío Toni always joins us for meals, not that he eats much. Sometimes he tells about what happened to him in the last few months. How the SIM raided one of the meetings he was at with friends, how he managed to get away, but rather than come home and put his family at risk, he went into hiding, going from one safe house to another, never sleeping more than a few hours a night. He's still real nervous all the time, jumping up whenever the door bangs or Lorena drops silverware on the floor. He's attentive to everything, noticing Lucinda's rash and Mundín's bitten nails. It's *una vergüenza,* he keeps saying, his jaw tensing, a shame that children can't be children anymore in this suffering country.

Papi is nodding little nods like those dogs with springs in their necks that people put in the back windows of their cars. "Democracy," Papi says, "but democracy is only the beginning. Education is the key."

Mami hushes them both with her eyes. We have to be careful of being overheard by someone on the SIM secret payroll. Lorena was recently caught "cleaning" the desk drawers in Papi's study.

Papi and Tío Toni are so brave. It makes me want to be like Joan of Arc, a courageous girl who heard heavenly voices. But unfortunately, unlike Saint Joan, I've yet to hear a voice tell me what I can do to help my suffering country.

*　*　*

"I hear there's going to be a big fiesta next door," Tío Toni says at dinner one night.

"Aren't you coming, Tío?" Lucinda seems surprised that our handsome uncle would pass up a party. He's a great dancer and extremely popular with the ladies.

"I think it's best if your *tío* doesn't say *pío*." Tío Toni laughs. Best to lay low. Besides, he hasn't been invited. Mr. Washburn has to turn in his guest list to the Foreign Ministry every time he has a gathering. It would look bad for the American consul to be hosting a man who has only just been pardoned by the government.

"I wish I could be there," he adds, winking at Lucinda. "I'd like to see that trail of broken hearts."

"Ay, Tío, don't start," Lucinda scolds, pretending to be disgusted.

"I mean it," Tío Toni persists. "You will be the queen of the ball."

I glance over at Lucinda, and I'm surprised at how pretty she is. Her dark hair is pulled up in a high ponytail, and her dimples show when she smiles. Lucinda reminds me a lot of the oldest girl on the *Mickey Mouse Club* show I've seen on the Washburns' television. "Hi, I'm Annette!" the girl calls out.

"And this *señorita* isn't far behind," Tío Toni says, winking at me. My uncle claims I've grown up in the months since he has been gone. In fact, I'm not a *señorita*, as I haven't gotten my period yet. But odd things are happening to my body. My breasts have swollen into two small buds that hurt if anyone bumps into me. I've also grown a whole quarter inch since Christmas. Maybe I'm not going to stay small forever, like poor Monsito, who never gets enough to eat.

Inside my heart, odd things are happening as well. By now, I'm almost one hundred percent in love with Samuel Adams Washburn. The one percent doubt has to do with what happened on Valentine's Day. I mean, what *didn't* happen. I didn't get a card from Sammy—but then, none of the girls got valentines from boys, that I know of.

Before Tío Toni leaves, he puts his arms around Lucinda and me. "I want my two butterflies to take care of each other," he says in a soft voice, squeezing our shoulders.

"We will, Tío," Lucinda promises, kissing my uncle. Then she leans over, brushes away my bangs, and kisses me!

On Lorena's day off, two men come over from the consulate to check the whole house for bugs. And I don't mean insects, either. The SIM like to hide little devices in houses so they can listen in on what you say. They might have planted some when they came for their raid . . . or someone could have planted some since then.

"Who?" I ask Lucinda. She spells out Lorena's name in English!

That afternoon, I overhear Mami talking to the canasta group on the patio. "The place is clean, thank God!"

"What about the girl?" someone asks.

Mami hired the recent graduate without checking her references because we desperately needed another maid to help Chucha. "She showed me her diploma from the Domestic Academy."

"Don't you know?" Mrs. Mancini whispers, looking over her shoulder. I pull back just in time from the doorway. "That place is nothing but a front for the SIM. They train those poor girls to be spies in households!"

Suddenly, I hear footsteps behind me. I jump. But it's only

Chucha! She leans forward and whispers one of her favorite sayings: "*Camarón que se duerme, se lo lleva la corriente.*" The shrimp who falls asleep is carried off by the current.

I guess if I'm going to spy, I'd better watch out for other spies—like Chucha!

The night of the party, we hear cars going up and down the driveway. Voices drift over from the neighboring yard, punctuated every now and then by the report of firecrackers going off in different parts of the city in honor of Independence Day. The early guests are starting to arrive.

Lucinda has taken her dress to the Washburns' so that she and Susie can get ready together. Mami is delayed in the kitchen, where she and Chucha and Lorena are frying extra batches of the Washburns' *pastelitos* for the party.

"When are we going over?" I keep asking. I know I'm nagging, but I'm dying to get all dressed up and have Sam see me.

"With patience and calm, even a burro can climb a palm," Chucha reminds me.

"Take this over, please," Mami asks Lorena when the first batch is done.

"Let me do it," I volunteer.

But Mami shakes her head sharply. "That's enough, Anita."

As soon as Lorena disappears down the shortcut path through the hibiscus hedge, Mami calls out, "Coast is clear!" Papi and Mundín slip out and join some men who have crossed over from the party to talk to Tío Toni. Tonight, I'm too excited thinking about my first grown-up party to ask Mami what is going on.

Finally, the frying is done. Mami and I dress quickly—she in her long black gown with the slit up one side so she can walk. When Chucha first saw it, she told Mami to take the dress back to the seamstress and have that rip sewn up.

I get to wear Lucinda's pale blue organdy she's outgrown but won't let me keep. Mami puts some lipstick on me, but I refuse the hairspray because Sam says that sprayed hair looks like an astronaut's helmet. As for Lucinda's old patent-leather heels I wore at Christmas, they no longer fit. But I've found some blue satin flats of Carla's that match the dress perfectly and are honestly much easier to walk in.

We cross over, Lorena and Chucha bearing the platters of *pastelitos*, Mami carrying the tray of sugared almonds to put inside the swan baskets the canasta group has prepared as party favors. We're headed the long way down the driveway, past the hibiscus hedge, Mami cautious in her spiked heels and tight dress that make walking on the dirt shortcut path too difficult.

Just ahead, a line of black Volkswagens crawls up the main driveway. Mami stops short. "Ay, *Dios*, I forgot my shawl," she says in a tense voice she tries to disguise. "Chucha, you and Lorena, go on ahead. Here, take this tray. We'll be right over."

"I'll get your shawl for you, Doña," Lorena offers. "I know where it is."

A look passes between Mami and Chucha. "You're not leaving me to carry all these platters!" the old woman snaps at the younger one. "Come along now, don't dawdle. The *pastelitos* are getting cold."

The minute they've gone a few steps, Mami grabs my arm and pulls me back behind the hedge of hibiscus. "Listen to me, Anita," she whispers fiercely. "I want you to run back to Tío Toni's *casita* and tell Papi and the others that Mr. Smith's friends are here. You hear me? Mr. *Smith's* friends. Hurry!" she says, practically shoving me on my way.

I've been wanting to hear a voice like the one Joan of Arc heard, and here it is! I run down the dirt path all the way to Tío Toni's pad. *Mr. Smith's friends are here. Mr. Smith's friends are here*, I say over and over under my breath—as if there's any chance in the world that I'm going to forget.

The men stand abruptly when they hear my footsteps, Tío Toni yanking something out from under his belt, Papi pulling Mundín behind him. But the minute he sees me, Papi calls out. *"Es mi hijita."* It's my little girl.

"Papi," I gasp, before he can scold me for the scare I've given them, "Mami says to tell you, *Mr. Smith's friends are here*." I don't know exactly what I'm saying—though, of course, I remember what Susie and Lucinda said about a Mr. Smith who likes pretty girls.

The effect of my words is instantaneous. It's as if one of the firecrackers that have been going off all day long has suddenly fallen in the center of the group. In seconds, the men take off, some with Tío Toni into the darkness of the back of the property, some following Papi and Mundín at a run toward our house.

When we reach our patio, Papi lets go of my arm. He holds up a hand, signaling everyone to slow down. He speaks in the tensest voice I've ever heard him use. *"Con calma, como si nada."*

Calmly, as if nothing is going on, we walk slowly down the path toward the Washburns' lit-up patio, where the party is in full swing. Elegant ambassadors with their fancy wives on their arms pick snacks off silver trays. Oscar and Sam, wearing bow ties, have been enlisted to take drink orders. Here and there, military men in fancy dress uniforms are looking up at the distant flashes of fireworks in the sky. Lucinda and Susie and their girlfriends sit on lounge chairs, their crinoline skirts spread around them like the petals of flowers. Young men surround them, as if drawn by the perfume of those flowers, closer and closer.

From their post by the buffet table, my mother and Mrs. Mancini are nervously scanning the crowd. They look relieved when they spot us coming back from the garden. Mami turns her head slightly, signaling to Papi. Men in dark glasses who look like the thugs who raided the compound months ago lurk at the shadowy edges of the patio.

What are the SIM doing here? Perhaps they've been summoned to protect the high-ranking military guests and ambassadors? I'm about to ask Oscar what he knows when there's a shout. "*¡Atención!*"

The party goes silent. The crowd parts as if a god is coming down among us. An old man, chest gleaming with medals, face whitened with pancake makeup, steps onto the patio.

"*¡Que viva El Jefe!*" a woman's voice cries out.

"Long live the chief," a chorus of voices echoes. *Boom, boom, boom*, the fireworks explode, lighting up the sky. For a moment, night turns into day as Mr. Smith lifts a small, spotted hand and gives us a weary wave.

six

Operation Maid

Mami and Papi are still in shock as we cross over to our house after the party.

"I can't believe it!" Mami is saying.

"Nobody was expecting him," Papi agrees. "Washburn got a call at the last minute. El Jefe wanted to drop in and congratulate the young lady. Imagine! How could he refuse? Washburn says before he could even think to come over and tell us to break it up, the SIM were at the door. If it hadn't been for our little messenger here . . ." Papi reaches out a hand and I take it.

I feel so brave and proud—even if the evening was a disappointment. I never did get a chance to dance with Sam. Mami made me stick to her side as if someone was going to pounce on me.

"We've let ourselves get careless!" Mami continues as we climb up the driveway toward our house. Tío Toni and his constant flow of visitors have to go somewhere else. "They're putting our children's lives in danger."

"Where can they go?" Papi argues back. "This is probably the safest place for Toni right now. For all of us."

Just then, we hear the clang of Lorena trailing behind us with an armload of empty platters. Mami always says that one thing Lorena never learned at the Domestic Academy is how *not* to make a racket.

"We have to find a way to let her go," Mami whispers to Papi. It won't be easy. We can't get on Lorena's bad side. Out of spite, she might report any number of curious things to the SIM. In fact, Mami has been bribing her with old clothes and tips and extra days off to keep her happy with our family. There is only one way to get rid of her, and that is to enlist Chucha's help in scaring the young woman. It's no secret to any of us that Lorena is really superstitious and squeamish. She won't wash her hair or cut her nails on Friday. She can't stand the sight of blood. She never sleeps faceup because she believes the devil will take her soul. She is deathly afraid of seeing the dead and has all kinds of charms pinned to her bra to keep a ghost from coming near. Needless to say, she is terrified of Chucha, who dresses in purple like a *bruja* and sleeps in a coffin.

Up ahead, Chucha stands at the door to her room, watching our progress. She must have crossed over earlier and turned on the lights to guide our way. Seeing her there, backlit, in her long gown, I feel that no harm will come to us as long as Chucha is around. Recently, she told me of a dream she had in which first Lucinda, then Mundín, then Mami and I sprouted wings and flew up into the sky.

"What about Papi?" I asked worriedly.

"Not everyone can be a butterfly," Chucha replied.

The morning after Susie's party, a black limousine with palace plates rolls up our driveway and delivers a bouquet of roses tied with red, white, and blue ribbons, the colors of our flag. The little card reads:

> *Para la linda Lucinda,*
> *flor de la patria,*
> *de un admirador.*

" 'For the beautiful Lucinda, flower of the nation, from an admirer.' " Mami flings the card to the floor as if it's contaminated. "I told you to keep that shawl over your shoulders," she scolds Lucinda. Poor Mami is so desperate, she has to find someone to blame.

Lucinda bursts out crying the minute she realizes the roses are from El Jefe. Her neck is more inflamed than I've ever seen it. "He's not going to take me away, is he, Mami? Oh please, Mami, don't let him take me away." Lucinda looks as scared as "the little baby" who sometimes crawls into bed with her at night.

Mami hugs Lucinda so tight, her hairband falls off. Normally, Lucinda won't permit Mami to give her these bone-crunching hugs. Now she collapses into Mami's arms. "That man gets near *mi señorita*, I'll cut off"—Mami glances over at me—"I'll cut off his hands," she vows.

"We'll protect you," I join in. My voice sounds small and silly even to me. Lucinda bursts out crying again. I feel like crying myself.

Midmorning, Susie and Mrs. Washburn drop in. They saw the palace limousine turn up our drive and wondered what was going on. "Goodness gracious," Mrs. Washburn says, putting the card back in its envelope. "That old goat!"

"Don't worry, Lucy," Susie reassures her friend. "Daddy won't let anything happen to you." I nod, hoping that what Susie says is true.

"I told her to wear that shawl." Mami starts up her scolding again.

"Carmen, honey, I don't think that shawl would have made a darn bit of difference. You can't hide your light under a bushel. And that old codger's got eyes on his"—she notices me. Why is everyone always looking at me when they are about to say interesting things?—"eyes on the back of his butt."

"Honestly, Mother," Susie says, rolling her eyes at Lucinda. But my poor sister is too scared to share in Susie's disgust.

"Where's Sam?" I ask. It suddenly strikes me that Sam has not come over with his sister and mom like usual.

"Young Master Sam and Master Oscar are probably sleeping off a mighty hangover. Yes, ma'am," Mrs. Washburn adds, nodding at my mother. "Those two boys got into the rum last night. One of those tin-medal generals bullied them that they had to learn to drink like little men. Mr. Washburn can't wait for Samuel Adams to recover from his hangover so he can get what else is in store for him today."

I wonder what else is in store for Sam today. Do the Americans punish their children by making them sit on a punishment chair, the way my parents once did? We've all outgrown that chair. In fact, it seems we've outgrown punishment altogether in the last few months. All we need to get back in line is one of Mami's desperate looks or Papi's stony-faced ¡No! that allows for no further argument or discussion.

When the phone rings, we all jump. Once, twice, three times, it keeps ringing until Lorena picks it up. In a minute, she is at Lucinda's door. "It's for la señorita," she calls out through the door.

"¿Quién es?" Mami calls back.

"Un señor," Lorena replies. As a graduate from the Domestic Academy, Lorena knows to ask for the name of a caller. Unless, of course, that caller is someone who needs no introduction.

Lucinda sinks back in her pillow and begins to sob again.

Mami stands to take the call, but Mrs. Washburn comes to our rescue. "Let me handle this." She opens the door and follows Lorena down the hall. "I'm sorry," we hear her say in her bad Spanish. "There's no one here by that name."

When Papi comes home from work at noon, Mami tells him what has been going on all morning. Papi is so upset, he won't eat his lunch even though it's his favorite, a *sancocho*, with leftover *pastelitos* from the party. He and Tío Toni go off to the back of the property, and a little later, Papi crosses over to discuss things with Mr. Washburn.

Meanwhile, the phone keeps ringing. Mami has instructed us not to answer it. As for Lorena, there's no danger of her interference. Mami has given her the rest of the day off. "I've been overworking you, and it's not fair," Mami said, stuffing a tip in the young woman's pocket and practically pushing her out the door.

Papi comes back from the Washburns' with news of a plan the consul has thought up. They are calling it Operation Maid. Friends in Washington who will be stationed in Colombia have been looking for someone who can teach their children some Spanish. Why not send Lucinda?

Mami won't have it. "My daughter's not going to be anybody's maid—"

Papi's reply cuts off all argument. "Would you prefer she be Mr. Smith's little *querida*?"

Mami doesn't say another word. It's decided. Mr. Washburn will request a special visa from the foreign ministry to send Lucinda to the States to help out his friend.

But Tío Toni isn't so sure the plan will succeed. The ministry will never disappoint Mr. Smith in order to please a mere consul.

"I say we take Smith down now!" my uncle insists. He paces the patio, lighting cigarettes he forgets to finish, flicking the butts into the ginger bushes nearby.

"The king must die," Papi agrees.

My mouth drops. They're talking about murdering El Jefe! I feel scared just thinking about what I've overheard. What if the SIM have a way to read people's minds?

"Let's not rush into this," Mami cautions. "El Jefe is many things, but he's not stupid. He won't refuse the consul. Remember, he really wants to win back the Americans so the embargo stops."

"We'll see," Papi says, as if he's struggling to believe what Mami is telling him.

For the rest of the day, I can't concentrate on anything. I just can't believe my own father would do something he's always taught me is wrong! Maybe saying the king must die was like the metaphors Mrs. Brown was always talking about? A figure of speech, not something that's actually true.

I corner Mundín in the hallway and ask him to please tell me what is going on. "Are Papi and Tío Toni really going to kill El Jefe—"

Mundín claps a hand over my mouth and looks around worriedly. "Don't ever say that to anyone!" His voice is so desperate, I burst into tears. He must feel bad about scaring me because he adds, "Everything'll be all right." I try hard to keep my mind on those words and on what Chucha dreamed—Lucinda, Mundín, Mami, and I, sprouting wings. Maybe she didn't see Papi because he went ahead, preparing our way in a country he is already familiar with?

In Lucinda's bedroom, everything is in disarray. Piles of matching blouses and skirts lie all over her bed. Even in the middle of an emergency, my older sister worries about what to wear. Finally, with Mrs. Washburn's help, Mami packs a small, sensible bag of what is necessary.

I stand by, as stunned as I was that November day when my cousins left. Even though it's only been less than four months, it seems so long ago. It's as if I've gone from being eleven back then to being really old now, at least as old as my grandparents, who are in their sixties. The thought of losing Lucinda to the United States of America, hard as she sometimes is on me, is too sad to think about. Not even the thought of falling in love with Sam is a consolation anymore. Overnight, all boys (except for Papi and Tío Toni and Mundín) have become totally gross. Here's an old lech flirting with my sister. Here are Oscar and Sam drinking liquor and throwing up. If only I could be Joan of Arc, cut off my hair and dress like a boy, just to be on the safe side. Or even better, if only I could go backward to eleven, instead of forward to thirteen!

Since it might be our last night together, Lucinda invites me to sleep in her room. I help her roll up her hair, and even when I don't get the rollers tight enough, she doesn't say anything. She also puts some of her pimple cream on my face, though I don't really need it—but then, neither does she.

Finally, Lucinda turns off the light and seems to go right to sleep. I try, I really do. But lying in the dark, I start seeing visions of El Jefe lying in a puddle of disgusting blood, and Papi and Tío Toni standing beside the body, and I feel sick to my stomach. Then I hear a sob. At first, I think it's mine, but it turns out to be Lucinda crying.

I reach out a hand and touch her shoulder. It feels strange to be comforting my older sister. And here she promised Tío Toni to take care of me!

"I just want you to know," Lucinda sobs, "that I . . . I . . . I'm sorry for anything mean I've ever done."

That does it. A loud sob bursts from me, too. Lucinda rolls over, and we hug each other until we have no more tears left. "We're going to look awful tomorrow," she says, laughing and crying both. What do I care? No one will see me. It's Lucinda who'll be meeting people in the United States she has to impress.

We talk in the dark, Lucinda telling me all about boys she likes and how many times she has been kissed. The first kiss she ever got, she was wearing her blue organdy dress, which is why she never would let me have it, even after she'd outgrown it. It's nice knowing she was being sentimental, not mean. I feel so sad to be losing my sister just when we're getting closer. Finally, we both fall asleep.

When I stir the next morning, my nightgown and legs feel damp. Oh, no! I think. I wet the bed! And here Lucinda has been treating me like someone her own age. Lifting the sheet, I gasp. There are bloody stains on my nightgown and on the bed!

My first thought is that I've been stabbed. But how can that be when nothing hurts anywhere? Maybe some horrible thing has happened to Lucinda? Maybe the SIM snuck into our house in the middle of the night and stabbed her in punishment for not taking Mr. Smith's phone call?

"Lucinda," I shake her awake. "There's blood. . . ."

"Go back to sleep," she says wearily. But then, my words must register because suddenly she is wide awake and sitting up. "Where?"

I lift the sheet and she looks down with a questioning expression. Then a knowing smile spreads on her lips. "Congratulations," she says, leaning over and kissing me. "My baby sister's a *señorita*."

I don't feel like a *señorita*. I feel more like a baby in wet diapers. And I don't want to be a *señorita* now that I know what El Jefe does to *señoritas*.

"Let's get you cleaned up," Lucinda is saying. She has gotten out of bed and is searching through a drawer. She finds a spare belt and shows me how to rig it up with a sanitary pad.

"Just please don't tell Mami," I plead. Mami will tell Papi, and right this moment, the last thing I want is a man knowing I've gotten my period.

"What'll we do with the sheets?" Lucinda asks, nodding toward her bed.

I know one person who will keep my secret. As soon as I've dressed, I make my way warily down the hall, a white bundle under my arm, trying hard to ignore the sanitary pad I'm wearing. How do girls ever get used to walking with this contraption between their legs?

As I pass Papi's study, I hear voices: Papi and Mami discussing something with Mr. Washburn. The consul must have come over first thing this morning with some news. The kitchen and pantry are deserted. Lorena hasn't returned from her night off. Out back, in the walkway between the house proper and the servants' quarters, Chucha is putting out her bedding to sun on the line. She glances at the bundle under my arm and guesses exactly what has happened.

"It's about time," she notes. Then, unfolding the sheets and glancing at the bloody marks, she adds, "This will do."

"Do what?" I ask. I know Chucha made Mami save all our bellybutton cords from when we were newborns to bury in the backyard. Does Chucha also do something with a girl's first menstrual blood?

"Mi secreto, tu silencio," she replies as usual.

I promise not to divulge her secrets, but for the first time, I ask her to return the favor. "Please don't tell Mami, Chucha, please."

She studies me for a moment, then nods as if she understands my desire for privacy. "Everything will be all right," she promises, echoing Mundín's words from the night before. "Mr. Washburn is already here with good news. Your sister is leaving today. *La amiga* Susie is going as well."

I feel relief to hear that my sister will be safe, even though it means Lucinda has to go away. It's like one of those operations where they save your life but take out some big part of you.

"You will be flying, too, one day soon," Chucha reminds me. "But right now, we have to get someone else out of the house." She glances over her shoulder at the door to Lorena's room. "Come with me."

She leads the way into her room, hung with purple cloths at the windows, a sweet, herbal smell in the air. We stop in front of a picture of a saint with a flickering votive candle in front of it. The saint isn't Santa Lucia because she doesn't have a little tray in her hands with her eyeballs rolling around. And it isn't Santa Barbara because she doesn't have a crown on her head and a tower behind her back. This saint has long hair and wears a red tunic and sandals and wields a huge sword above a disgusting-looking dragon with a tiny human face. "San Miguel," Chucha intones, "protect this house from all enemies. Expel the bad. Bring all to safety who dwell within. Amen."

I pray along with her, and then—as Chucha likes to say—the work of God that must always be done by man begins. Between the two of us, we push and drag and tug that coffin out the narrow door, upend it, turn it around, and put it in the room next door. We set it up in front of the neatly made bed, lid open, with Lucinda's bloody sheets spilling out the sides. It looks like a dead person just crawled out, leaving his bloody winding sheet behind.

I admit I feel mean participating in this scheme—but I also understand that our lives are in danger. A tip from Lorena could wipe us out. It's *so* unfair to have to live in a country where you have to do stuff you feel bad about in order to save your life. It's like Papi and Tío Toni planning to assassinate Mr. Smith when they know that murder is wrong. But what if your leader is evil and rapes young girls and kills loads of innocent people and makes your country a place where not even butterflies are safe? I feel sick to my stomach all over again just thinking about all this.

After we are done, Chucha closes herself up in her bedroom and begins to pray to San Miguel again. On my way back through the house, I bump into Mr. Washburn coming down the hall from Papi's study. I turn my face away, trying to avoid his eyes. He's the first man I've encountered since getting my period. I'm sure he can see right through my pants to the belt and pad I am wearing.

"I have some good news, Anita," Mr. Washburn is saying. "Your sister's visa came through."

I glance up at those kind blue eyes that are exactly like Sam's eyes, and my disgust begins to fade away. Mr. Washburn is risking his life to help my family as well as my suffering country. Here is another man (along with Papi and Mundín and Tío Toni) to add to the list of good guys I might be able to trust again.

Back in Lucinda's bedroom, Mami is explaining that Lucinda

has only gotten a visitor's visa, so she doesn't have to be a maid, after all. The new plan is that she will accompany Susie on a visit to her grandparents in Washington. Once she is safely out of the country, Mr. Washburn will figure out how to keep her there.

"By the way," Mami asks, glancing down at the bed, "what happened to your bed?"

"Chucha stripped it this morning," Lucinda says, looking over at me. "She said she knew I'd be leaving today."

"*Esa Chucha es un cuento.*" Mami smiles, shaking her head. Chucha is something else.

Just then, we hear a cry from the back of the house. Lucinda and Mami look at each other worriedly. What can it be?

We don't have to wait long to find out. Minutes later, Chucha is at the door with the news that Lorena is packing her things and also leaving the house.

seven

Lying Policemen

Papi whistles his special time-to-go whistle from the hallway. He's driving me and Mundín and Sam to school. I'm lingering in Lucinda's bedroom, watching her pack and repack her small suitcase as if there's going to be a test on it when she lands in the United States.

Mami comes to get me. "Papi's waiting."

"I want to stay until Lucinda leaves." In fact, I don't want to go to school at all! My eyes are all red from crying and my tummy's upset.

But Mami insists. "Anita, we've got to make everything look as normal as possible. Even I'm not going to the airport with the Washburns," she reminds me. "Now come. You'll be late."

I turn to face Lucinda, and we collapse in each other's arms, sobbing. She finally pulls away, trying to be the brave one. "Don't forget," she says.

I nod, though I honestly can't remember what it is I'm not supposed to forget.

Nothing feels right today. Just past our house, the police have stopped a car, and the passengers are getting out with their hands in the air. Papi's jaw tenses up. I slip the crucifix around my neck into my mouth—something I've started doing when I need extra good luck.

Papi slows often for the speed bumps that have been appearing all over the city. Everyone calls them "lying policemen," which makes me think of dead policemen buried underneath the street. I suppose with all the crazy stuff happening, my imagination is going wild.

My biggest fear is that something I've done or said will cause us to be killed. What if Lorena tells the SIM about how I kept a diary hidden under my pillow that I erased every night? I mean, that has to sound suspicious. *Please please please,* I pray to the little crucifix in my mouth.

We stop at the high school to drop off Mundín. He must know how bad I'm feeling because he turns around in the front seat and ruffles my hair like he used to when I was a little kid. "Maybe later we can go for a drive?" he offers. Mundín is allowed to take Tío Toni's hot rod up and down the driveways in the compound.

His being so nice makes me want to cry. I don't dare open my mouth, afraid a sob'll burst out.

"I'll go with you if she doesn't want to," Sam pipes up. All the way to school, he's been talking about what a great time he's going to have now that his bossy older sister is leaving. It makes me feel even sadder that his feelings are so different from mine. But then, the more I think about it, that's the way it's always been.

"I have some rather sad news to report," Mrs. Brown says first thing in class. I am so numb already, I don't think I can feel any more sadness. But when she says that the American School is going to close its doors temporarily, it's like the last straw Chucha says broke the donkey's back. Even though I complain about school, I really don't want the last normal thing in my life to stop. I lay my head down on my desk.

"Are you feeling ill, Anita?" Mrs. Brown is by my side. "You're going to have to answer me, dear, so I know what to do." Her voice is sweet and coaxing. She crouches down beside my seat.

I don't seem to have the energy even to lift my head and say, "I'm fine."

"I think we'd better have the nurse look at you," she says, taking my hand.

I don't resist. I stand and walk with her. As we cross the front of the room, Charlie Price makes a circle motion in the air to Sammy, who grins as if he agrees.

I feel like screaming, *I AM NOT CRAZY!* But instead, I swallow that scream, and suddenly it's very quiet inside me.

The nurse calls Mami, who appears at school in Tío Toni's hot rod, since Papi has the other car. She looks glamorous, with a kerchief over her head and dark glasses like a movie star. When she takes them off, I see that her eyes are red, too. She must have been crying after Lucinda left for the airport.

"What's wrong, *amorcito?*" she asks.

I want to tell Mami the truth, how I've gotten my period, how I'm already lonely for Lucinda, how I feel just awful that my father has to kill someone for us to be free, how I'm scared about what's going to happen to us, but all the words seem to have emptied out of my head. Finally, I remember one. "*Nada,*" I say.

"Nothing? Are you sure?" Mami peers at my face. "She looks pale," she tells the nurse. "I better take her home to bed."

The minute we get in the car, Mami turns to me. She looks terrified. "You didn't say anything about Lucinda, did you?"

I shake my head. Can't she see that I'm not saying anything to anybody?

*   *   *

I spend the rest of the day in bed. Chucha brews me a tea of *hierbabuena* leaves that makes the flutter in my chest and the cramps in my tummy go away. Later, Mundín stops in. The high school is closing, too, he reports. Maybe tomorrow, if I feel better, we can drive around the compound. He keeps biting his nails as he talks. I know how he feels. Except instead of biting my nails or breaking out in hives like Lucinda, I seem to be forgetting words.

I'll start to say something, and just like that, I'll go blank over a word. It doesn't even have to be an important or hard word, like *amnesty* or *communism*, but something easy, like *salt* or *butter* or *sky* or *star*. That makes the forgetfulness even scarier.

Maybe Charlie is right and I *am* going crazy?

Please, please, please, I pray. The crucifix around my neck is in my mouth so often the features on the little Christ face are starting to wear off.

As soon as Papi gets home, he comes and sits on the edge of my bed. Unlike Mami, he doesn't ask me a dozen questions. He smiles tenderly and strokes my hair. His eyes are the saddest in the world.

"One day . . . in a time not too far in the future . . . ," Papi begins, as if he's telling me a bedtime story, "you're going to look back on all this and think, I really was a strong and brave girl."

I shake my head. *I'm not so strong or brave*, I want to say.

"Oh yes, you are. I know you are," he insists, reading my thoughts. He tips my face up by the chin so I'm looking straight at him. I feel as if he's hypnotizing me. "I want my children to be free, no matter what. Promise me you'll spread your wings and fly."

What on earth are you talking about, Papi? I want to ask him. It's spooky to hear Papi sounding like Chucha! But I can't seem to get the words out of my head and down the chute that connects them to my mouth.

Mami pokes her head in the door. "How's she feeling?" she asks Papi, as if I'm not in the room at all. She comes over to the bed and touches my forehead with the back of her hand. "I think it might be the mumps that's going around."

Papi shakes his head. "It's not mumps," he says. He turns back to me, still waiting for a promise I'm not prepared to give him yet.

Every night now, the men meet at our house on the back patio. They've grown extremely cautious, using code phrases all the time, but they let one little thing slip by them. The patio swings around the house to a private nook where they like to sit talking, and that nook is directly beside my bedroom window. Every night as I lie in bed, I can hear their hushed voices, even as I'm losing mine.

Tío Toni is always there, and Papi, and sometimes Mr. Washburn, who brings Wimpy. Mr. Mancini has stopped coming because the group decides that he can provide a safe house in case of trouble. I don't know what that means except that it's probably why, now that our American school has officially closed, Sam and Mundín and I go over to the Mancinis' house for our lessons. Mami and Mrs. Washburn and Mrs. Mancini—in fact, the whole canasta group—are not about to let their kids grow up dumb *brutos* just because of a dictatorship. All in all, I think there are about twelve of us from different grades, now thrown together, learning addition and algebra, "*Cielito Lindo*" as well as "Twinkle, Twinkle, Little Star."

Mundín and I always ride over with Sam in the consulate car, as it's less likely to be stopped at the guardposts beyond the lying policemen. There are now all kinds of checkpoints and curfews. One day, we ride to school and every other person on the street and in their cars is wearing black. When Sam asks Mundín about it, my brother says these people are voicing a silent protest. Sometimes, I think of my growing silence that way: voicing a silent protest.

More and more people are getting arrested, too. I hear the men talking one night about this one drugstore where the owner, a sympathizer, will sell you a pill you can take if you get caught by the SIM. It kills you instantly; that way you can't be tortured and reveal the names of other dissidents. Every time I help Chucha with the laundry, I check all of Papi's and Tío Toni's pockets, just in case they've forgotten their pills there. I plan to flush them down the toilet, all but one, which I'll keep for myself. In case the SIM take me away, I'll slip that pill in my mouth, and then my crucifix. Maybe God will forgive me for committing suicide to avoid being murdered?

So much for trying to be brave and strong like Joan of Arc!

"*¡Ya esto no se puede soporta!*" Tío Toni is saying. This has got to stop. They've been waiting around for weeks for a delivery of what they call "the ingredients for the picnic." Tonight is no different from any other night, except that their voices are starting to sound more desperate.

"The Americans are playing with us, that's what you don't realize," Tío Toni continues. I know he's talking to Papi, who says that after the way Washburn helped with Lucinda, he trusts *ese caballero* with his life.

"It's not Washburn, it's his people in Washington dragging their feet," another voice is saying.

"*El pobre* Washburn," Papi agrees. Poor Washburn. "He's on his way out."

So the Washburns are leaving to join Susie in Washington! As for Lucinda, she's now in *Nueva York* with my grandparents and cousins, sending me postcards that show buildings so tall even Chucha is left speechless. Lucinda signs her name "Marilyn Taylor," after her two favorite actresses, Marilyn Monroe and Elizabeth Taylor. According to Mami, Lucinda knows we can get in trouble for corresponding with a person who hasn't returned when her visa expired.

The door opens a crack, and a dagger of light cuts through the darkness. It's Mami, checking up on me. She usually waits until all the men are gone, but maybe she wants to catch me before I fall asleep. "Are you up, *amorcito?*" she calls into the room. Of course, had I been asleep, her calling out would have woken me. I turn on the three monkeys lamp so that she feels invited in.

Mami sits down beside me on the bed. She chuckles when her eyes fall on the silly lamp. Three monkeys—one with his hands over his eyes, one with his hands over his ears, and a third with his hands over his mouth—stand in a row under a palm tree with a green shade that covers the lightbulb. It's one of the things we inherited from the García girls when they left the country. Carla and I always made fun of this awful lamp that one of our aunts with poor taste once gave them. When Lorena broke my bedside lamp cleaning one day, Mami got this one out of the storage closet.

Mami is shaking her head at the monkeys. "We can move Lucinda's lamp in here if you want." I've always pretended to hate the lamp, rolling my eyes theatrically. But really, it's kind of comforting to have the three monkeys lamp Carla and I made fun of together beside me.

"Wouldn't you like that?" Mami is giving me that pleading look she wears these days when I won't talk much. "Ay, Anita, tell me what's going on. You look so skinny and sad, and you're too quiet to be Mami's *cotorrita.*"

I hate when Mami worries about me and starts calling me her little parrot and treating me like I'm five again.

"You miss your sister, don't you? And now I have—not bad news, just a change."

"The Washburns are leaving." My voice comes out hoarse, I guess from not using it much anymore.

"How did you find out?" Mami looks puzzled. "Sammy doesn't even know." She continues studying my face for clues as to what I'm feeling, her eyes filling. "Maybe we've told you too much? Maybe we made you grow up too fast?"

"Mami, don't . . ." I've forgotten the word for *cry.* I put my little crucifix in my mouth. Sometimes, doing so helps me remember the words for what I want to say.

"I'm sorry." Mami is sobbing now. She reaches for me and holds on so tight, I'm reminded of the hug she gave Lucinda the day El Jefe's roses arrived. "I wanted you to have a childhood," Mami sniffs, wiping her tears.

I think of reassuring her by telling her that my childhood is over anyway. That I've already gotten my period. But the voices outside my window have grown animated. Mr. Washburn and Wimpy have arrived.

"It's bad news," Mr. Washburn is saying. "They're not going to send any more ingredients for the picnic."

"I told you they'd back out on us," Tío Toni reminds the group.

"I'm sorry, fellas," Washburn says. And he really does sound sad. "I'll deliver what I have on hand in a few days at our drop-off."

"Our usual place," Wimpy confirms.

Mami looks like the monkey with his hand over his mouth. I don't know if she's upset at the news she just heard or at suddenly realizing that I've been listening in on the men's secret meetings for months. She leans over my bed and angles the jalousies open. "*Señores,*" she calls out, "everything can be heard from this room."

The gathering goes absolutely silent, and then Papi walks over to the window and peers in over Mami's shoulder to where I sit on my bed.

"No wonder" is all he says.

The men move their meetings back to Tío Toni's *casita*, even though it isn't as convenient as the patio with the shortwave nearby in Papi's study tuned to Radio Swan. Oscar says that Swan is a new station that broadcasts important bulletins by exiles who want to liberate the island. Everyone in the whole country is listening in, even though it's illegal to do so. I've heard the men say that there are dissidents everywhere—even among the armed forces and policemen and cabinet members—just waiting for a signal that El Jefe is out of the way.

One time I try turning on the shortwave, hoping to hear that we're free. But I don't know which knob is for the volume and the radio blares for a minute. Mami hurries in. "What are you doing, Anita? Come along now and help me get the card table out."

Mami wants me by her side at all times when I'm not at the Mancinis'. With only Chucha left in the household, I've taken over lots of little jobs, including helping out when the canasta group comes over, cleaning ashtrays, refreshing glasses of lemonade.

"Hey, sweetheart," Mrs. Washburn calls me over to her side one afternoon. She puts her cards facedown on the table. "Are you going to miss your pal Sam?" Although Mr. Washburn won't be leaving until late June, Mrs. Washburn has decided she and Sam will join Susie in Washington soon. It's April, and Sam has already missed too much of the school year. And Susie is proving to be a handful for her poor grandparents.

Mrs. Washburn puts her arms around me and squeezes hard. "Why haven't you been coming over to visit? Did you and Sammy have a little squabble?" She winks at Mami. Obviously, they've been talking about me. "Maybe you'll come visit us in Washington?"

I know I'm being rude, but I can't come up with the words to answer her.

"Will you come and visit us sometime?" Mrs. Washburn persists.

I can feel Mami's eyes prying the words from deep inside. I try to pull them out myself. But they won't come. All I can do is shake my head.

"Young lady," Mami corrects. No matter how worried she is about me, she still won't stand for rudeness. "That's no way to turn down an invitation."

But Mrs. Washburn waves Mami's scolding away. She gives me another tight squeeze. Can't she see that I'm not a little girl anymore? That I have breasts that hurt when she does that?

"Thank you, Mrs. Washburn," my mother coaches.

"Thank you," I echo in the small voice I've learned for being polite.

Sam still comes over, but it's not to visit me anymore. Now it's to hang over the hood of Tío Toni's hot rod with Mundín, fixing up the motor. Tío Toni has promised Mundín the car as soon as my brother gets his license when he turns sixteen. What I always wonder is, how good can a car be that always needs some repair?

The special feelings I once had for Sam have definitely faded. Now he seems like a regular boy, with his hair too white as if it's been left in a bucket of bleach overnight, his eyes a dull blue. He and Mundín are always talking about cars. Chucha and I will pass by the carport and overhear them discussing the carburetor and brake pads, points and plugs. I'll repeat these words to myself, as if by doing so I'll somehow be able to understand my older brother and my former love a little better.

Sometimes, when Mundín and Sam are out working on the car and Mami and her friends are playing canasta on the patio, it seems as if things might be going back to normal. Suddenly, I'll think up a dozen things to say to Chucha about something I saw in one of Mrs. Washburn's *Life* magazines or a plan for a hairdo that'll make me look older. But then something happens to remind me that we're not safe, and my words slide away again.

Thursday morning, we are on our way to Oscar's house for class, Sam and Mundín and I. His chauffeur has the day off, so Mr. Washburn is driving. He has a stop to make downtown at Wimpy's anyway.

Wimpy is over at the Washburns' a lot these days. I've heard Sam tell Mundín that Wimpy is really an undercover agent for the United States. That's why Mr. Washburn has been bringing him to the secret meetings at our house.

Today, traffic is heavy. Probably, El Jefe's car is expected down the main avenue, which means cars will be backed up until his motorcade passes. We inch forward at a crawl. Beside me, in the backseat, Sam is looking uncomfortable, squirming this way and that.

Suddenly, the car ahead of us brakes, and as we brake, too, the car behind rams into us, and the trunk flies open.

Mr. Washburn is out of the car in a flash. From their guardpost, two policemen, who have seen the accident, head down the block toward us. Sam turns pale at the sight of soldiers approaching, wielding machine guns. He opens his door and hurries out to join Mundín and Mr. Washburn at the back of the car. I'm right behind him.

"No problem," Mr. Washburn is saying to the driver who has run into our car. "It's understandable, bad *tráfico*." He's talking too fast, as if he's the one who rammed into a car, his hand trying desperately to push down the trunk that has flown open. But the dent in the trunk won't let the latch catch.

"Allow me," one of the policemen offers, strapping his weapon over his shoulder and rolling up his sleeves.

"*No, no, por favor,*" Mr. Washburn insists, waving him away from the trunk. "All that is needed is a piece of rope."

The driver of the car behind us runs off to get some rope he has stored in his trunk. Meanwhile, the second policeman heads back to his guardpost to make out his report.

"You will dirty your sleeves!" Mr. Washburn is still arguing with the remaining policeman about helping with the dented trunk. But the policeman is insistent. He steps forward and lifts the lid to inspect the damage.

I cannot describe what I see, for the words slide away from my memory. In fact, no one says a word. We stand for a long moment, looking down into the trunk of that car. The driver, who has arrived with the coil of rope, glances down and his eyes grow wide.

Jolted from their sugar-cane sacking, barrels poking out, the ingredients of the picnic have spilled out across the floor of the trunk. The guns were on their way to the drop-off point, the mission disguised as a school ride for us kids.

The policeman must see them, too. But all he does is reach for the rope from the terrified driver and loop one end into the lid and then through the bumper and knot them tightly together.

"You better get that fixed," he says quietly to Mr. Washburn when he's done.

"¿Todo bien?" his buddy calls from their guardpost.

"Everything is fine," the policeman lies, waving us on our way.

Back inside the car, Mr. Washburn's hands are shaking so badly, he has trouble turning on the ignition. I smell urine, as if someone has peed in his pants. My heart is thundering in my chest. I pull out my chain and put the little cross in my mouth, but I can't come up with the words for a simple prayer of thanks.

eight

Almost Free

"He's coming!" Oscar yells from the nursery room we use as our classroom. We've been playing hide-and-seek with his three little sisters. Since Oscar is It, I wonder if he's trying to trick us into coming out of our hiding places. "Hurry up or you'll miss him!"

I look at the clock in the hallway, and sure enough, it's five-fifteen. El Jefe will be walking down from his mother's mansion, past Oscar's house next to the Italian embassy, all the way to the *avenida* by the ocean. Every evening of the week, he follows the same routine. Oscar says El Jefe is really strict about his schedule and does things right on the dot, not a moment before or after. He is superstitious that if he's off by a minute, something awful will happen to him.

I race down the hall so I can catch a glimpse of El Jefe, surrounded by his throng of bodyguards and important people from his cabinet. The first time I saw this afternoon parade, I was surprised to recognize several men from the group that gathers at our house every night to talk about getting rid of El Jefe.

I don't say so to Oscar. I don't say much even at school these days. Many times, when we play hide-and-seek to keep his little sisters entertained, I won't come out of my hiding place when I hear "Ally ally oxen free!" But like Papi, Oscar seems to understand my silence and goes on talking to me anyway.

"El Jefe's not wearing his jewelry today." María Eugenia, the oldest of the three little sisters, has joined us at the front window.

"It's not jewelry, it's his medals," Oscar corrects.

"Why can't they be jewelry?" María Eugenia protests. "They're gold."

"There's twenty soldiers," María Rosa pipes up. She just started learning numbers, and so everything she sees, she counts up. She's the youngest of the three little girls, all of whom have María as part of their name. Mrs. Mancini is really devoted to the Virgin Mary, Oscar has told me. Even *he* has María in his name, Oscar M. Mancini. At school, Oscar always refused to say what his middle initial stood for.

"Why does he have so many soldiers?" María Josefina, the middle sister, wants to know. All three little girls are now crowded at the window.

"Because," Oscar answers shortly.

"Because what?"

Curiosity runs in the family.

"Shhh, he's going to hear you!" Oscar warns. The three little girls fall silent. Oscar has already told them that if they get caught spying, they'll be taken out on the street and shot.

"That's strange. He's wearing his khaki today," Oscar points out. El Jefe always wears his white uniform, except on Wednesdays, when he heads for his country home at night. Then he wears a green khaki outfit. But today is only Tuesday.

"He probably has a new girlfriend," Oscar guesses. El Jefe keeps all his girlfriends out in his country house, where his wife never goes. Otherwise, she would surely murder them.

I shiver, remembering how El Jefe spotted Lucinda at Susie's party and started courting her with roses. Quickly, I draw back from the window. What if El Jefe looks up and sends his SIM up to get me? "So, you are the girl who never cries!" he would greet me.

No, señor, I rehearse my reply. *I am the girl who hardly talks anymore.*

After El Jefe passes by, I stand a while at the window, looking up at a glint of silver in the sky. The daily Pan Am flight is departing for the States. The García girls left on that flight, as did my grandparents, uncles, and aunts and their families; then Lucinda and Susie; and finally, a few days ago, Sam and his mom.

Oscar comes up beside me. The little girls have been called to their baths. We are alone in the nursery. "Are you sad because of Sam leaving, Anita?"

It's sweet of Oscar to care. But I don't know how to tell him that I haven't been spending all that much time with Sam. In fact, the last time we saw each other alone was when Sam came over to say good-bye. Sam talked on and on about how excited he was to be going back to the United States. He handed over a present, a little Statue of Liberty paperweight that I was sure his mother had picked out.

"Thanks," I managed to murmur. I wanted to say something more. After all, Sam was my first love. There was a time when my heart would play jump rope when I saw him crossing over to our house. But those feelings had completely fizzled out. Sam had grinned when Charlie made fun of me. Why hadn't he defended me? Maybe he just hadn't been brave enough to stand up for me? Not being brave is easier to understand than being plain mean.

"It's scary being the ones left, don't you think?" Oscar is saying.

I look down at the fists my hands have formed without my even telling them. Suddenly, I'm so grateful to Oscar for admitting he's scared, too. Now I don't have to feel as if I'm going crazy all by myself.

"You know what Papi says?" Oscar asks. His voice is real quiet as if we're in a secret place together. "You can't be brave if you're not scared."

I know *exactly* what he means! Oscar sure seems a lot older and wiser than when he used to ask Mrs. Brown a lot of questions. I smile back at him.

He leans toward me, and for a moment I think he's actually going to whisper a secret in my ear. But instead, his lips touch my cheek. It's an odd moment to be getting my first kiss!

Shortly after that, Papi comes by to pick us up. He honks the horn for us to come quickly. Usually, he gets out of the car and visits with Doña Margot, Mrs. Mancini's mother, while Mundín and María de los Santos, Oscar's older sister, finish up their game of Parcheesi. Doña Margot, who lives with the Mancinis, chaperones María de los Santos whenever boys come to visit. That means she hangs around María de los Santos to make sure nothing happens, rocking in her rocker and falling asleep after a while. Mundín, who just turned fifteen, has a terrible crush on Oscar's sister, who's a whole year older than he. She wears her hair down her back in one long braid, which she unbraids and rebraids whenever she gets nervous. At least her nails are intact.

Doña Margot stands on the balcony and waves for Papi to come in.

Papi waves back. "*No puedo, Doña Margot. Tengo un compromiso.*" He can't come in. He has a commitment. Maybe one of his after-dinner meetings with Tío Toni and his friends.

I gather my things and race downstairs to the car. Usually, I hurry to beat Mundín so I can sit in the front next to Papi. But today I have to get away from Oscar. It isn't that I'm sorry he kissed me. I just can't find the words for the mixture of confusion and pleasure I'm feeling.

Sitting in the car, I'm sure Papi can tell that a boy has kissed me. But Papi seems distracted, turning on the radio, then turning it off, honking the horn a few more times before Mundín finally appears at the door. From the balcony, María de los Santos waves her languid good-byes as my brother climbs in.

On the drive home, Papi keeps forgetting to slow down for the lying policemen. "Are you going out tonight, Papi?"

He doesn't answer me right away, which is unusual. I speak so rarely these days that when I do, people make a point of paying attention to me.

"Eh, Papi?" I ask again.

Papi turns to me with that if-looks-could-kill look in his eyes, but the minute he realizes who I am, the look shifts, and he smiles. "What was that, Anita?"

I try again, but the words have slipped from my mind.

"She asked if you were going out tonight." It's Mundín from the backseat. Just last Wednesday, Papi and Tío Toni's friends gathered at our house, talking in excited whispers. Then everyone got into their cars and drove off. Later that night, I heard the Chevy coming back, doors closing, and then Papi and Tío Toni explaining something to Mundín and Mami about Mr. Smith not showing up at the picnic site.

"Going out? Yes, yes, I'm going out tonight," Papi says absently.

"I heard he was wearing his khaki today," Mundín notes.

Papi looks in the rearview mirror and nods.

* * *

We drive through the compound gates, past the empty guardpost and the deserted García house. A few days ago, Mr. Washburn was issued revised orders to vacate the compound and have no further dealings with any dissident elements. He has moved to the consulate downtown, where he'll be staying until his return to the States in late June.

Our driveway is crowded with cars parked at screwy angles in a hurried way. Just inside the door, someone has turned the portrait of El Jefe to face the wall. Tío Toni and his friends are gathered in the living room, talking in excited voices. Mami rushes out to the entryway to greet us, her eyes wide and frightened. She whispers something to Papi, who gives her the same nod he gave Mundín in the car.

Mami's eye falls on me, and her face struggles for composure. "How was school today?" she asks, but she doesn't notice my blushing or wait for an answer. One of the men comes back in from his car with a heavy sack in his arms. "*Aquí no,*" she snaps, motioning with her head toward Papi's study. She doesn't want the man unloading his gear in front of me.

Mami's still trying to keep stuff from me because she worries about my being so quiet and thin. But for weeks now, I've sensed that some big thing is about to happen, big enough to distract Mami from fussing as much over little things, which is fine with me.

I'll come back from school and find her at the typewriter in Papi's study. When I ask her what she's typing, she says, "Just some work for your father." One time, right before she burned the trash in a coal barrel in the yard, I found a page all crumpled up. I uncrumpled it and read CALLING ALL CITIZENS on top—the rest was like a Declaration of Independence in Spanish, listing the freedoms that the country would now enjoy. "All citizens are free to express their opinions, to vote for the candidate of their choice, to receive an education. . . ." I felt like I was reading something George Washington might have written, only it was typed instead of handwritten, and thought up by my papi and his friends instead of by a bunch of white-wigged colonial men.

Mami also worries a lot about Mundín. Now that he's fifteen, he won't be treated as a minor if the SIM start rounding people up. Mami has had several discussions with Papi about sending Mundín to New York to my grandparents, but Papi reasons with her that there is no way Mundín will be granted permission after Lucinda never returned when her visa expired. And such a request might tip off the SIM that something big is about to happen.

"Children, tonight an early supper," Mami is saying, as if Mundín and I are six and nine instead of twelve and fifteen. "Then off to your rooms."

"I'm going with Papi," Mundín announces, pulling himself up straight as if he is twenty-one instead of fifteen.

"¿Usted está loco?" Mami asks him. Are you crazy? She's using the formal usted as she always does when she's angry with us. "Mundo!" she calls to my father, who has gone ahead into the living room and is greeting all the men. Papi comes back out and Mami explains what Mundín is proposing.

Papi puts his hands on Mundín's shoulders. All he has to say is, "If anything should happen to me . . . ," for Mundín to bow his head obediently.

After a spaghetti supper that none of us can eat, Mami, Mundín, and I go into Mami and Papi's bedroom to listen to the radio and wait. Radio Caribe, the government station, is having a recitation contest, but most of the poems are about El Jefe, so Mami turns it off. I think about my cousin Carla winning her eraser in the shape of the Dominican Republic at the children's recitation contest last year. But I can't remember the winning poem she recited. Perhaps it, too, was about Trujillo.

Every few minutes, Mami or Mundín goes to the window and checks to see if any of the cars have come back. I have lots of questions in my head, but I can't find the words, nor do I want to make Mami any more nervous by asking them.

We sit on the big bed, paging through the *Life* magazines Mrs. Washburn left for us when she moved out. There are lots of pictures of the handsome President Kennedy and his pretty wife, Jackie, who looks a little like my beauty-queen aunt, only paler and less made up. There are also pictures of the astronaut the Americans have put up in space. He's curled up in a capsule like an unborn baby. The capsule's name, *Freedom 7*, is written in big block letters on its side. I imagine him out there, spinning farther and farther away from the planet Earth, as lonely and scared as I feel deep down inside myself.

The knock at the door makes us all jump. It's Chucha. Do we want our beds turned down? Mami nods absently.

"I'll help," I offer, wanting to get out of that tense room. As Chucha and I fold up Mundín's bedspread, I tell her about the astronaut flying in outer space.

Chucha narrows her eyes as if trying to see something that has been a long way off but is now coming closer. "Get ready," she whispers.

"For what?" I gasp. I wish Chucha wouldn't talk mysteriously when I'm so nervous!

Chucha lifts her arms and pumps them up and down, her purple sleeves billowing. "Fly, fly free," she reminds me.

Of course. Chucha's dream: first Lucinda, then Mundín, and then Mami and me flying in the sky. I had pictured us taking off to the United States of America, angel wings on our shoulders. Now I imagine us crammed inside a space capsule, headed for who knows where.

Just then, Chucha and I hear the cars honking their way up the driveway, doors banging shut, excited voices in the front of the house. Out in the hall, Mami and Mundín are racing to the door as the men come trooping in, brandishing guns. "*¡Que vivan Las Mariposas!* Long live the Butterflies!" they greet us. Papi picks up Mami and twirls her around, then sets her down and does the same to me.

"Is it true? Is it really true?" Mami keeps searching Papi's face to make sure it's safe to celebrate.

Papi's face is flushed and happy. "It is true, Carmen, true, true, true. After thirty-one years, we are free again!"

Tío Toni, who has been trying to get someone on the phone, comes back to the entryway. His face is grim. "No one can find Pupo," he announces to the men.

"What do you mean no one can find Pupo?" Papi asks, then hurries away to the phone and begins dialing some numbers.

Who's Pupo? I want to ask. The desperate look on all the men's faces means that Pupo is someone really important they have to find.

"If that bastard double-crossed us . . . ," one of the men is swearing, but another man hushes him so they can hear what Papi is saying.

"Did he say where he was going or when he might be back?" Papi's voice is calm and casual, a friend trying to get ahold of a friend to chat. But he's winding the phone cord around and around his hand, as if he means to strangle his fingers. "No, no message, nothing important. I'll call back."

When he hangs up, Papi's face is as grim as Tío Toni's. He begins issuing orders. A couple of men are to go by Mancini's house. Someone else is supposed to do something else, and someone else is supposed to go somewhere else and tell someone something. I can't keep it all straight because of all the shouting and running around, plus my heart is beating so loud! I put my hand on my chest to calm it down and look over at Papi, hoping he'll glance my way and wink and tell me everything's going to be fine. But he's reminding the different groups before they take off that the most important thing is to find Pupo and bring him here to view "the evidence." It seems only Pupo, whoever he is, can give the signal that will make everyone fall in line.

Mami's face is a china cup someone has dropped on the floor. "And what happens if you don't find Pupo?"

Papi glances over at El Jefe's portrait, which was turned to the wall earlier in the evening. With all the ins and outs, someone must have brushed against it, and the picture has twisted itself back around. "If we don't find Pupo, it's every man for himself," Papi explains, looking from one face to another. Everyone seems to understand.

Papi heads for the bedroom, Mami clinging tearfully to him. I wait in the hall until they come out again, Papi patting his shirt pocket, a gun handle visible under his belt. At the front door, he kisses Mami, then he kisses me, avoiding our eyes, as if he doesn't want us to see how worried sick he is.

I want to say good-bye to him, but the words are stuffed inside my mouth like a gag keeping me from talking. From the entryway, I watch as the cars start up, their different lights aimed in all directions, like searchlights going crazy. Across the way, the García house is dark. If only someone were next door to help us now! For the first time since my family and then the Washburns left, I feel angry at all of them for deserting us.

Mami suddenly turns, looking around frantically. "Where's Mundín?" she asks me, as if I'm keeping tabs on my older brother. "Mundín!" she calls. Her desperate voice rings out in the empty house. "Mundín!"

Chucha is locking up the garage and hosing down the driveway, which seems a strange thing to be doing in the middle of the night. When she hears Mami calling, she turns off the hose and comes back in.

"Where's Mundín?" Mami asks her.

"I saw him get into the first car," Chucha replies.

"Ay, no!" Mami wails. She races to the phone, but in her desperation, she dials several wrong numbers before she gets the one she wants. "Doña Margot," she cries out, "is Mundín there?"

She must hear what she wants to hear because her face relaxes. "Under no circumstances let him out of your sight!"

When she hangs up, Mami wears a cross look on her face. "When this is all over, I'm going to give that boy the punishment of his life."

Chucha shakes her head slowly. "No, Doña Carmen. It's too late for that. Why, Mundín is already a man! He has flown the nest."

I look out the door and down the dark driveway. The whole flock of our family has fled. Only Mami and Chucha and I are left.

nine

Night Flight

For the rest of the night, we wait and wait for Papi's return. Chucha goes off to her room to light her candles and pray to San Miguel. I try praying, too, but as I kneel beside Mami, all I can think about is how to escape if the SIM come to our door. No suicide pill for me! I'm going to fly, like Papi and Chucha said. I want to be free!

The best idea would be to run to the back of the property, past Tío Toni's *casita*, and take the back road to the crowded marketplace. We could probably find someone to carry a message to Mr. Washburn at the consulate. Monsito! Maybe if Mami gave him all the money in the safe, he'd help us out? It's strange to think that now we are the beggars, but instead of asking for alms, we're asking for help so as not to lose our lives.

Lose our lives! The words grip my heart. Will the SIM really kill us? Will they torture me if I don't talk? How can I explain to them that it's not personal, that I'm not talking to anyone? That I forget words even when I try not to?

I look over at Mami, hoping she'll say that everything's going to be all right. But her hand is shaking so badly that she can't even finger the beads on her rosary. Mami's scared, too! Oscar said you have to be scared to be brave. I just have to stay one step ahead of being scared. If it's just a small step, maybe I can do it.

Where is Oscar right now? I'm wondering. Is he awake and

scared and trying to be brave, too? I touch the place on my cheek where he kissed me. Maybe after being Joan of Arc for the revolution, maybe then I can go back to being a normal girl and fall in love with Oscar?

Finally, Mami and I decide to try and get some rest. As if my room might be safer now than hers, Mami lies down beside me on my bed. We keep Mundín's transistor radio tuned to the one official station, hoping Pupo will make his announcement. But all they play is a program of organ music that reminds me of High Mass at the cathedral and has the same effect. I drop off to sleep.

Later on, I'm awakened by the sound of sirens. "It's nothing," Mami says soothingly, but her hand on my back is ice-cold.

I turn in the dark and look toward where I think her face might be. The words for what has been uppermost in my mind all night tumble out. "Mami, are we going to be okay?"

She doesn't say anything for a long time. I wonder if she has fallen asleep or if she is also beginning to lose her memory of words. Finally, she replies, "Like Chucha says, we're in God's hands now."

"Who's Pupo, Mami?" I ask. The way the men were talking, our lives are not in God's hands but in Pupo's.

"Pupo is the head of the army. He was supposed to announce the liberation. It looks like he failed us."

But won't lots of other people help? I want to ask. I'm thinking of the policeman who didn't denounce Mr. Washburn when he spotted the guns in the trunk of the car; the thousands of people who, Tío Toni has said, will be brave because of the Butterflies. But the words are again sinking down to the bottom of my memory.

"Without the army, we're lost." Mami begins sobbing. "And to think we were almost free."

I reach out and stroke her back, like she just stroked mine.

The organ music plays on, like a funeral that will not quit.

The rest of the night is a blur as I fall in and out of sleep, everything running together, the dreaming and the waking, the García sisters standing in the snow in a place called Central Park in the snapshot they sent us; the eraser in the shape of the Dominican Republic; Sam bouncing up on his trampoline but never coming down, until he is an astronaut tumbling away into outer space; Oscar's little sisters hanging out the window, their heads like three shiny black bowls; Oscar leaning over but instead of kissing me, branding Wimpy's eagle tattoo on my cheek; Chucha dragging her coffin into Lorena's room; the blood on Lucinda's sheets becoming the blood Chucha tried to hose down from the driveway tonight; then the sounds of cars coming back, wheels squealing, doors banging shut, calls left and right; the scared whispers, the rushing-around steps, Tío Toni's voice, and Papi's and Mami's; and then the endless silence through which I am falling down, down, down—

Chucha is shaking me awake. Sunlight is streaming in through the jalousie windows. Before I can ask her what's the matter, gangster men in their dark glasses storm into the room, thrusting their guns here and there in the corners of the closet and under my bed, in search of something they cannot find.

Chucha and I clutch each other and watch the men pulling open drawers, throwing my clothes on the floor. Soon another bunch of men come into the room, pushing Mami in her nightgown before them. "Traitors!" they shout.

Mami rushes to me and holds me so tight, I can hear her heart pounding in my head. I'm too terrified even to cry.

When they're done with our room, they nudge us with the barrels of their guns into the living room. A tall, skinny man with a thin mustache sits in Papi's chair, directing the operation. Men run in and out, reporting their finds. They refer to him as Navajita, little Razor Blade. I don't want to think how he came by that nickname.

"Have a seat," Navajita offers, as if this were his house, not ours. He stretches his mouth like a rubber band, showing us his teeth. It takes me a second to realize that he's smiling.

We sit and wait, cringing at the sound of glass breaking, things smashing as his gang ransacks the house and the grounds.

"We found El Jefe!" a SIM agent comes shouting into the room. The skinny man stands abruptly, as if there's a spring under him. His profile is as sharp as a razor blade. "In the trunk of the Chevy," the agent explains, "locked up in the garage."

"Take them in," Navajita orders. The SIM agent hurries out, shouting orders.

From the front window, we can see a swarm of black Volkswagens, engines starting up. Papi and Tío Toni, hands tied behind their backs, are being pushed toward one of the waiting cars.

Mami races to the window. "MUNDO!" she cries out.

My father's head jerks around before he's shoved into the car.

"Where are you taking them?" Mami wails.

"Where they took El Jefe," Navajita replies grimly.

Soon the other agents who have been scouring the compound gather in their cars, driving over the lawns, leaving a trail of smashed-up flowers and muddy wheel marks. I try to catch a glimpse of Papi or Tío Toni, the backs of their heads or a flash of their profiles, some little bit of them to hold on to in my memory. But I cannot remember which car is theirs or whether it has already gone ahead to a place where I don't want to imagine what is waiting for them.

The minute they disappear, Mami begins making phone calls, trying to find someone who can help us. But everybody seems to have taken flight. Spooky funeral music keeps playing on the radio. Wherever Pupo is, he has not been found to make his announcement that El Jefe is gone. Instead, the SIM and Trujillo's son and brothers seem to be in charge, and they are going to make the whole country pay for the murder of El Jefe.

We huddle together in that wrecked house, not knowing what to do with ourselves. Everything that used to be in a drawer or on a shelf is smashed and broken on the floor. Mami's jewelry, my charm bracelet, the silver in the velvet-lined box in the dining room, and Papi's car have been confiscated, now "property of the state." Even the wishing coins at the bottom of my grandparents' pond have been fished out. The last time the SIM raided us, they were very polite compared to this. We're in real trouble now.

Mami and Chucha and I start to clean up, but Mami breaks down. "What's the use?" she sobs. I keep right on, helping Chucha, trying to stay one step ahead of being terrified. But the panic is stirring inside me, a big black moth of scaredness flapping around inside my chest that can't get out. I sweep and dust and clean extra hard, as if that's going to set it free.

Finally, Mami manages to reach Mr. Mancini, who comes right over, shaking his head at the mess the SIM have made of our house.

Mami is trying to control herself, but she keeps dabbing at her eyes with one of Papi's handkerchiefs. Every time she blows her nose, she sees the monogram and that gets her started crying again. "We've got to do something. Ay, Pepe, please, God, we've got to do something."

Mr. Mancini bows his head, as if he doesn't want Mami to see the bad news written all over his face.

"Ay, Pepe, they'll murder us all, *uy, Dios.*" Mami is sobbing uncontrollably.

Mr. Mancini escorts her to a chair and offers her his handkerchief, since Papi's is all wet and balled up. "*Cálmese,* Carmen."

"*Por favor,* Pepe, *por favor,* we've got to find Washburn."

"What we must do at the moment is find you a safe place. The SIM will be back, believe me. If they can't get the confessions they want, they will come after the wives and children. They're already rounding up the boys in some families."

"Mundín!" Mami's hands are at her throat.

"Mundín is fine," Mr. Mancini reassures her. "Now you two ladies get a few things ready, *prontísimo.* You are coming with me." His eye falls on Chucha, who's standing by, listening to all this.

"Chucha, I suggest you close the house and go off to your people."

"*These* are my people," Chucha replies, crossing her arms.

"Anita," Mami says, "go with Chucha and collect some of your things."

"And bring some of Mundín's things as well, Chucha," Mr. Mancini adds, giving Mami a small nod.

While Chucha packs a bag for Mundín next door, I try to gather up some clothes, but my room is such a mess, I can't even find two matching socks. A big heap lies on the floor: school clothes and dresses and torn blouses all thrown together with panties and shoes. Papers are scattered everywhere; my books and pencils have been emptied out of my schoolbag; even the diary I stashed away months ago on a shelf in the closet has been hurled near the door. Seeing everything I own thrown around like trash makes me want to give up. I tell myself, *Be brave, be strong.* But when I see that pathetic little monkey hand from the smashed lamp sticking out from inside one of my tennis shoes, I collapse, sobbing, on top of all my stuff.

"*¡Vengan!*" Mr. Mancini is shouting from the entryway for us to come.

I try to stand but I cannot move. The same paralysis that has attacked my voice now seems to have taken hold of my legs.

Chucha hurries into the room. She takes one look at me and begins stuffing clothes in the laundry bag that once hung behind my door, a rag doll's face on a hanger with her body an empty sack. When she's done, she pulls me to my feet and wraps her arms around me as if she is filling me up with her courage.

"*¡Ya! ¡Ya!*" It's time. Fly, fly free! She yanks up my laundry bag and, at the last minute, scoops up the diary and stuffs it inside. Pushing me before her, we race out the door, my legs gaining strength as I fly through the house to the waiting car, Chucha urging me on.

Anita's Diary

June 3, 1961, *Saturday, time of day, hard to say*

We are finally settled in and Mami has said, go ahead, write in your diary as much as you want, we're in trouble already, maybe you can leave a record that will help others who are in hiding, too.

Mami now speaks in spurts of panic instead of sentences. I tell her that all I want to do is keep a diary, not save the world.

I don't want any freshness here, Anita, I've just about had it, I'm up to four Equanil a day, that's sixteen hundred milligrams, I can't take it.

You see why I need this diary.

June 5, 1961, *Monday morning—Mami's showering in the bathroom next door*

I can only write a little bit at a time, as I don't get much privacy around here, even though it's just me and Mami in the walk-in closet in the Mancinis' bedroom. When the Mancinis lock their bedroom door, we can visit with them in their room and do things like take a shower. Otherwise, we have to stay in the closet.

Last night in the middle of the night, Mrs. Mancini shook us awake and whispered, I don't know which one of you is doing it, but I'm afraid you don't have the luxury of snoring in this house.

Our sounds have to sound like their sounds.

June 6, 1961, *Tuesday, early—or so it seems from the light streaming in the bathroom window*

Mrs. Mancini says it's a good thing she has always been in the habit of locking their bedroom door in order to get some privacy. Also, she has always cleaned the master bedroom herself, as the help have enough to do what with five kids. Besides, she doesn't trust anyone since she learned of the undercover training at the Domestic Academy. So the Mancinis' habits make their bedroom as safe a hiding place as any private residence can be right now.

The Mancinis have this kind of strange house like an apartment. The first floor is basically a large garage and laundry room and kitchen. They live on the second floor, since it's cooler up here with a gallery running all along the back and stairs going down to the garden.

From their bathroom window, I have a bird's-eye view of the grounds of the embassy. But unlike a bird, I can't fly free . . . except in my imagination.

Later, evening

According to Mr. Mancini, loads of people are being arrested. The whole town of Moca was imprisoned because one of the conspirators comes from there! El Jefe's son, Trujillo Junior, says he will not rest until he has punished every man, woman, and child associated with the assassination of his father. Actually, Mr. Mancini says that people are secretly calling it an ajusticiámiento, which means bringing to justice, the way criminals have to face the consequences of their evil deeds.

I feel so much better thinking that Papi and Tío Toni were doing justice, not really ~~murdering~~ ~~killing~~ hurting someone. But still . . . just the thought of my own father—

Have to go. One of the little Marías is calling at the bedroom door.

June 7, 1961, *Wednesday afternoon, a cloudy day, I can tell rain is coming*

Once the Mancinis go out, we have to stay quietly in the closet and can't move around or use the bathroom. (We have a chamber pot, but you'd be surprised how noisy peeing is, and how messy in the dark.)

Only two human beings in the house know we are here, Tío Pepe and Tía Mari (they insist I call them that now), and their two teensy Yorkshire terriers. Thank goodness Mojo and Maja remember me from school and Mami from the times the canasta group met here, so they don't bark at us. No one else knows. Tía Mari says it's going to be a job keeping a secret in this curious family. But it's just too dangerous right now to tell anyone where we are.

It is so strange to be in the very same house as Oscar, and he doesn't even know! Every time Tía Mari or Tío Pepe mentions his name, I can feel my face burn. I wonder if they notice my special interest?

The emergency procedure is, if the SIM start a search or anyone comes into the bedroom (besides the Mancinis), we slip into the bathroom, where there are two narrow closets; Mami goes in one and I go in the other, all the way to a crawl space in back, and we stay there and pray we are not discovered.

June 8, 1961, *Thursday, right after supper, in bathroom*

During supper tonight, Tía Mari turned on Radio Caribe kind of loud. Meanwhile, Tío Pepe tuned his shortwave radio to Radio Swan real low since that station is still illegal, and he and Mami and Tía Mari leaned forward listening closely to the "real" news. It was like night and day, what each station was reporting.

CARIBE: The OAS is here to help the SIM maintain stability.

SWAN: The OAS is here investigating human rights abuses.

CARIBE: Prisoners praise treatment to OAS investigation committee.

SWAN: *Prisoners complain of atrocities to OAS investigation committee.*

CARIBE: *Consul Washburn has been recalled.*

SWAN: *Consul Washburn has been airlifted by helicopter to protect his life.*

Both stations agreed on one thing: The plot did not work. Pupo, the head of the army, just wasn't there to announce the liberation over the radio, and instead, Trujillo Junior has taken over, and it's a bloodbath out there. The SIM are doing house-to-house searches. Over 5,000 people have been arrested, including family members of the conspirators.

I wanted to block my ears and not listen to this stuff!

Whenever I feel this way, I start writing in my diary so there's another voice that I can listen to. A third radio, tuned to my own heart.

So I snuck off to the bathroom with my diary, and soon enough, Mami was calling me, saying it was rude for me to be off by my-self, come join them and be sociable, but then Tía Mari told her to let me be, that it's a good thing that I'm writing, that ever since I started keeping this diary, I'm talking a lot more.

It took her saying so for me to realize it's true.

The words are coming back, as if by writing them down, I'm fishing them out of forgetfulness, one by one.

June 9, 1961, Friday—evening

Mami has heard from Tío Pepe that Mr. Washburn is back in Wash-ington and pushing to get Papi and Tío Toni on the OAS list of prisoners interviewed, as their lives are then much safer. Once the OAS has a name on record, it's harder for the SIM to get rid of that individual.

Mami and Tía Mari have begun praying a rosary to the Virgin Mary every night to take care of all the prisoners, but most especially to take care of Papi and Tío Toni.

I always kneel with them. But even though I'm talking again, I can't seem to fish the words for an Our Father or Hail Mary out of my brain.

June 10, 1961, Saturday, late night

The electricity goes on and off all the time. Tía Mari bought Mami and me little flashlights. Tonight, a total blackout again. So I'm writing by the light of this tiny beam.

I never know exactly what time it is anymore—except when the siren sounds at noon and then again at 6 for curfew. The Mancinis don't have an electric clock in their bedroom because it would never tell the right time anyhow. The kind you wind drives Tía Mari crazy because it tick-tocks too loud. She says she feels like someone is timing her life.

The truth is, when you live in such close quarters, you find out the most private things about people—like Tío Pepe always having to wear white socks to bed or Tía Mari tweezing little hairs from her upper lip.

I wonder what they've noticed about me? How I stroke a spot on my left cheek whenever I'm feeling scared or lonely?

June 11, 1961, after supper, second Sunday in hiding

Sundays are especially hard, as that was always the day of our big family gathering. But we were reduced to just the Garcías and us, then just us, then just us minus Lucinda, and now it's even less than a nuclear family, just Mami and me, like survivors after a bomb drops, a fallout family.

Every day, I ask Mami about Papi and Tío Toni. But on Sundays, I probably ask her more than once. (No, not "countless times," like she accuses me of!)

Today, I promised myself I wouldn't ask her even once. But by evening, I couldn't stand it anymore. Mami, I said, just tell me if they're okay.

She hesitated. They're alive, she said, and started crying.

Tía Mari pulled her into the bathroom, and meanwhile I was left alone in the bedroom with Tío Pepe. We were quiet for a while and then he said, Anita, one must think positively. That is how the greatest minds in history have survived tragedy.

I felt like reminding him I'm not one of the greatest minds, but Tío Pepe is so smart, maybe his advice is worth a try?

I close my eyes and think positively. . . . After a while, a picture pops into my head of Papi and Tío Toni and me walking on the beach. I'm real little, and they're holding me between them and swinging me out over the waves like they're going to throw me into the sea, and I'm giggling and they're laughing, and Papi is saying, fly, mi hijita, fly, like I am a little kite that is catching the wind!

Then, like on a birthday, I make a wish: that Papi and Tío Toni will soon be free and that we will all be together again as a family.

June 12, 1961, Monday night, bathroom, about ten o'clock

Sometimes, I try to think of my life in hiding as a movie that will be over in three hours. It makes it a lot easier to put up with Mami's nerves!

So here's the scene every night when I want to write after lights-out:

SETTING: Dark inside of closet. Mother on her mat, not the most comfortable of beds, but a lot better than sleeping in prison or in a coffin!

ACTION: Girl feels for diary and flashlight under her pillow. Absolutely silently, she begins to slip out of the closet.

MOTHER: (whispering, loud enough to wake up sleeping couple in bedroom beyond closet) Remember, the Mancinis are asleep!

GIRL: I know. (Rolls her eyes in the dark, makes disgusted face, which, of course, mother can't see. Girl goes into bathroom, props flashlight on back of the toilet, and begins writing. Screen goes blurry and scene of what she's writing unfolds before our very eyes!)

Back to my diary—

*I want to write down everything that happened the night that Tío
Pepe rescued us from the compound—not that I'm likely to forget. I
don't think I've ever been so scared!*

*Mami and I crouched down in the back of Tío Pepe's Pontiac with
some sacks over us. Good thing, too, since the streets were crawling with
tanks. When we got to the Italian embassy, Mundín was already there,
and though Mami had sworn that she was going to kill him, she was so
pleased to see him alive and well and biting his nails that she just hugged
him and kept touching his face and hair. Poor Mundín looked like he had
suddenly turned from fifteen to fifty, his eyes glazed over with the horrible news of Papi and Tío Toni being taken away.*

*Meanwhile, Tío Pepe and the Italian ambassador came up with
a plan.*

*Since Mundín was most at risk, being a guy, he'd stay at the
embassy, as it's off-limits to the SIM if they're obeying rules anymore. But the place was so packed with refugees seeking protection, we
couldn't all stay there. So Mami and I were moved next door to the
Mancinis', which is not as safe. (Private residences do not have immunity privileges.) The plan is to get us all out of the country as soon as a
way can be found. Meanwhile, we have to lay low, not a peep from us,
as the SIM close in with their house-to-house searches.*

*When we got to the Mancinis' bedroom that first night, Tía Mari
showed us "the accommodations." Here is the dining room, she said,
pointing to her bedside table with magazines, and here is your bedroom,
she added, showing us the walk-in closet, then crossing the narrow hallway, here is your bathroom–living room–patio. She was trying to make
us smile.*

I started unpacking, and what a surprise to find my diary among my things! Then I remembered Chucha scooping it up and stuffing it in my laundry bag.

Ay, how I miss Chucha!

June 13, 1961, *Tuesday evening*

Tío Pepe says he drove by the compound today and the whole place was crawling with SIM. He heard through Radio Bemba, which is how people are referring to gossip, Radio Big Mouth, that the compound is now a SIM interrogation center. It makes me sick just to think what might be happening in my old bedroom.

What about Chucha? I asked. The thought of anything happening to Chucha . . .

Chucha is fine! Tío Pepe assured me. It seems that the day after he evacuated us, Chucha also left the compound. She wandered into town on foot, to Wimpy's, and has gotten a job there sweeping out the aisles, which is near impossible to believe. But Wimpy is one of Tío Pepe's contacts, so maybe Chucha feels that by being there, she is close to us. Who can tell?

Just the thought of Chucha at Wimpy's makes me smile.

June 14, 1961, *Wednesday morning, after breakfast*

Poor Tía Mari has to think of meals on top of everything else!

For breakfast, she always fixes Tío Pepe's tray first thing, before the cook is up, and carries it to their bedroom. So that meal is never a problem. Tía Mari just brings some extra waterbreads and marmalade and cheese and a pot of coffee and one of milk, and fresh fruits. She locks the door, and Mami and I slip out of the closet and eat breakfast, taking turns drinking out of one cup while Tía Mari and Tío Pepe share the other one.

As for supper, Tía Mari and Tío Pepe used to eat out in the dining room, but now, with the excuse that they want to listen to the news quietly in their bedroom, they bring their trays in here and we all eat off the two plates.

The problem is the big midday meal, as the family always eats together in the formal dining room. So what Tía Mari does is hide a plastic bag under her napkin on her lap, and she serves herself lots of food and eats slowly so that the little girls and María de los Santos and Oscar are excused long before she is done, and then quick, she scrapes her plate into the bag for us. It's not the most appetizing meal, a bag of mixed-up food, but when I think—which I don't want to—of what Papi and Tío Toni and the other prisoners are eating, I feel grateful and make myself eat so Tía Mari doesn't have to worry about getting rid of leftovers. (Mojo and Maja can only eat so much.)

Tío Pepe likes to tease Tía Mari that she has gotten so good with that plastic bag, if she ever needs a job, the SIM would surely hire her!

June 15, 1961, Thursday evening, already two weeks in hiding!!!

Earlier this afternoon, I was in the bathroom writing and I heard the three little Marías playing out in the yard. I felt such envy for them, enjoying the warm sun on their skin and the blue sky above.

Then I started thinking how Papi and Tío Toni might not even have a glimpse of sky and fresh air or a bite of food and all my positive thinking went out the window. I stroked my cheek, but that didn't help, either. I burst into tears. So much for the girl who never cried.

Mami caught me crying and began scolding, what is the matter with you, Anita, you're going to have to make an effort, please, you're too old for this.

Which made me cry even more.

Tía Mari pulled me into the bathroom and shut the door and whispered, Anita, you have to understand that your mother is under tremendous pressure, tremendous pressure, and so take that into account, and just keep writing, don't stop. Stay calm. Pray to La Virgencita.

My brave and beautiful niece, she added, hugging me.

June 16, 1961, Friday, after supper

Believe it or not, we get mail here!

Mundín writes out notes that he gives to the ambassador, who gives them to Tío Pepe, then we answer back by reverse method. It seems so strange that we should be writing back and forth when we're only a house away! Mundín won't say where exactly he is hidden in case the note should fall into the wrong hands, but he tells us he is fine, though very worried about Papi and Tío Toni. Today's note was just to me. I guess from his hiding place, Mundín caught a glimpse of María de los Santos sitting on the gallery with some young fellow, and he wants to know what I know.

I couldn't believe that Mundín was thinking about a girlfriend at a time like this!

But then . . . I'm thinking a lot about Oscar! As Chucha would say, the hunchback laughing at the camel's hump!

Tonight at supper, I'll drop a question about María de los Santos and see if the Mancinis volunteer any news of a boyfriend.

Mojo and Maja are making it hard for me to write—they climb up on my lap and chew at my pen. They look like two little waterfalls of hair, with a pink and a blue ribbon tied in a teensy pigtail on top of their heads.

Stay calm, I say to them. Keep writing, I say to myself.

June 17, 1961, Saturday night

Another scene from the movie of my life in hiding:

117

SETTING: *Girl and mother sitting in bedroom with husband and wife who are hiding them. Radio they have been listening to is turned off.*

GIRL: *(very innocently)* How is María de los Santos?

WIFE: Muy bien, *she is fine*, gracias *to* La Virgencita María.

GIRL: *Does she have a boyfriend?*.

WIFE: *(shaking her head)* When hasn't that girl had a boyfriend?

HUSBAND: *(looking up from shortwave radio, alarmed)* What's this? I didn't know you were allowing María de los Santos to have gentlemen callers.

WIFE: *(hand on her hip)* Allowing her? Who can tell that girl what to do? And where have you been that you didn't notice? Even the Chinese in Bonao know this.

(Soon, a full-blown disagreement is in progress. Mother and girl slip back into closet, and mother turns on girl.)

MOTHER: Look at what you started, Anita, I hope you're satisfied, such nice people, after all they have done for us.

(Girl keeps her mouth shut—someone has to keep the peace around here!)

June 18, 1961, *Sunday, late afternoon, sunny and bright*

My least favorite day . . . but today has been tolerable because *Tía Mari* invited Mami's old canasta friends for a Sunday barbecue. Of course, none of them know we are hiding here. But Mami has been so depressed that Tía Mari thought that just seeing her old friends secretly from the window would lift her spirits. It turns out that the whole canasta group are wives of supporters of the plot.

So why aren't they in hiding, too? I asked Mami.

Their husbands aren't directly involved, Mami explained. And we're in the most trouble because El Jefe was found in the trunk of Papi's Chevy.

118

Suddenly, it struck me that for a whole night, we were living with a dead body in our garage! It seemed so spooky, as well as dumb. Why would Papi and Tío Toni leave El Jefe's body lying around where the SIM could find it if they searched us?

The plan was to bring Pupo over to the house, Mami explained some more. Pupo had said he wouldn't start the revolution until he saw the dead body.

Usually, Mami starts to cry or gets upset with me when I ask her about all this stuff, but today she was the calmest I've seen her since we came into hiding. We took turns peeking out the high window in the bathroom, standing on the toilet. Mami reported on everyone she saw, Ay, pero Isa has gotten so thin, and look at Maricusa, she's cut her hair, y esa Anny is going to have twins.

When it was my turn, my eye was caught by a young man, off by himself, reading. Suddenly, I realized it was Oscar! Maybe it was from not seeing him for several weeks, but he seemed a lot older and very handsome. I kept watching him, every time I had a turn.

I've decided that I want to read more myself. I've been here almost three weeks now and all I've done is page through Tía Mari's magazines, play cards with Mami, listen to the radio, and write in my diary. Reading would make the time pass and take my mind off gloomy thoughts about what is happening to Papi or Tío Toni or us.

So I asked Tía Mari if she'd get me a book out of our old classroom. Which book? she wanted to know.

I shrugged and told her to get me anything she thought I'd like.

June 19, 1961, Monday night

Tonight, Tía Mari said, oh dear, I keep forgetting to get a book for you from the children's library. Here's one to start. And she gave me this book about the life of the Virgin Mary.

I tried to read some of it, but it was not very interesting.

Instead, I experimented with some new hairdos in the mirror, wondering what Oscar would think of a young lady with her hair pulled back in a ponytail.

June 20, 1961, Tuesday, late night

I talked to Tío Pepe about how I want to read more, and he said it was an excellent idea. He told me all about famous people in prisons and dungeons who did incredible stuff, like this nun way back in colonial times, who I guess wrote tons of poetry in her head, and the Marquis de Sade, who wrote whole novels, and someone else who worked on a dictionary, and another person who came up with some new kind of printing press. It was real inspiring, but not for me. I think I'll just stick to reading some books and writing in my diary.

Tío Pepe said that one thing all these famous prisoners found while they were locked up was that it was important to keep a schedule so as not to go crazy. Right then, remembering how Charlie Price called me crazy, I decided to draw one up and try to follow it every day.

Anita de la Torre's Schedule in Hiding:

MORNING:

Wake Up—Slip out so as not to wake Mami and touch my toes (20 times) and do waist exercises (25), plus the ones that Lucinda taught me so my breasts will grow (do 50 of those).

Shower and Dress—Brush my teeth for at least a minute so as not to end up toothless like Chucha, shampoo hair twice a week, and definitely do not spend the whole day in my pajamas or muumuu! Tío Pepe said the Marquis de Sade put on his powdered wig and morning jacket while he was locked up. Also, British lords used to dress in their white linens in the jungle and look at how long they ruled the world. I was going to remind Tío Pepe how El Jefe was real finicky about what he wore, too, and look at what a monster he was . . . but I decided I better keep my mouth shut.

During Breakfast—Try to learn one new thing from Tío Pepe, who must be a genius, as he knows about everything and speaks five languages perfectly.

After Breakfast—read good book (once Tía Mari remembers to bring me one), write in diary, try not to be bored, as Tío Pepe says boredom is a sign of the poverty of the mind—definitely do not want that!!!

NOON:

Lunchtime—Try to keep my stomach from growling before Tía Mari comes back with her hidden lunch bag, try to be nice about the eggplant squashed up with the rice and beans and leftover chicken (always dark meat, my least favorite) because, as Mami says, beggars cannot ask for _cebollitas_ with their _mangú_. (But I don't like onions with my mashed plantains!) Most of all, try to be nice to Mami.

AFTERNOON:

Free Time—Write in diary, talk with Mami about happy times in past. Tía Mari says this will really help improve her spirits. Try not to think about the tanks we keep hearing rolling down the street or the gunshots from the direction of the national palace, the dead quiet once curfew sounds at six.

NIGHT:

Eat Dinner—Usually the best meal, as Tío Pepe has to have his pasta once a day, which is my favorite food, too. Tío Pepe says I must have Italian blood in me. And, of course, that gets Mami and Tía Mari started on the Family Tree.

After Dinner—Listen to Radio Swan, try not to think of the sad news, of the 7,000 arrests, of the bodies thrown off cliffs to the sharks, of the army generals in their tanks shooting at neighborhoods where they think people are hiding, and instead . . . think positively! Join in discussions, think positively! Write in diary, look through Tía Mari's magazines, anything to avoid bad thoughts that might drive me crazy.

<u>Sleep</u>—Lights out around 10 P.M., but I can stay up in the bathroom reading or writing, provided—Mami does love a lecture—that I am very quiet, so as not to bother the Mancinis. Listen politely, try not to roll eyes and make disgusted face at Mami when she gives this lecture every night.

<u>Before Going to Sleep</u>—Think about Tío Toni and Papi on the beach, try not to think of bodies thrown into the sea, think positively, think of the sand and wind in my hair, and Papi saying, Fly, and Tío Toni laughing as they swing me up in the air.

X X X X X
X X X X

(one mark for each day I missed writing in my diary!!!)

June 30, 1961, *Friday, bathroom, very hot night*

I know, I know, it's been nine days and I haven't written a word.

I just couldn't after the fright we had the night I wrote up my schedule.

What happened was just awful!!! I was getting ready to cross back from the bathroom to the closet to bed when I heard someone moving around in the yard. The night watchman had already made his rounds at 10 P.M. or so, and this was after 11 P.M.

So I woke up Mami, who "never sleeps a wink," but I always seem to find her fast asleep, and we woke up the Mancinis, who turned Mojo and Maja loose on the gallery, and they scampered off and down the steps into the yard, barking and growling, and then there were gunshots, and Tía Mari was screaming from the gallery, MOJO! MAJA! but no answer, and Tío Pepe was trying to drag her back inside, while also hurrying into his dressing gown as there was now loud knocking downstairs at the front door.

We went into emergency procedure—Mami and I slipped into the bathroom closets and back into the crawl space—one of the boards is loose and it made a terrible Whack!!! sound—scared us half to death! We waited for what must have been 20 minutes but seemed forever. My heart was pounding so loud, I thought surely it could be heard throughout the house, and then, oh my God, I remembered I had left my diary on the back of the toilet when I rushed to the closet to wake up Mami! I didn't dare sneak out to get it and I didn't dare tell Mami because she would just die of one of her nerve attacks right then and there.

In a little while, Tío Pepe was back, and we all sat on the floor of the closet, and Tío Pepe told us the story.

The SIM had come to the door to say they had been called by the embassy because there were intruders on the grounds. (A lie!) It turned out the SIM agent in charge recognized Tío Pepe, whose brother-in-law, Dr. Mella, had saved his little daughter's life after a ruptured appendix. Anyhow, when Tío Pepe invited them inside to search the house, this grateful man said that would be unnecessary. Tío Pepe stood talking to them a little longer at the door and then they left.

Tía Mari quieted while Tío Pepe told the story, but then she started to cry again about Mojo and Maja.

The next morning, the night watchman reported the two dead dogs.

Poor Tía Mari was just crying and crying. Mami and I felt terrible, as it was our fault that this happened. And I felt doubly terrible leaving my diary out in the open! What if the SIM had come in and found it there? I could have cost us our lives on account of my carelessness.

For days, I wasn't able to write a single word. The third radio was turned off. But then, I started thinking, if I stop now, they've really won. They've taken away everything, even the story of what is happening to us.

So, tonight, I picked up my pen and, sure enough, I've been writing my heart out even if my hand is shaking.

July 1, 1961, Saturday morning

Two resolutions for the new month:

#1: Try to write something every day!

#2: Keep diary hidden at all times!!! At night under my mat, and during the day when we roll up the mats, in the pocket of Tía Mari's fur coat that she wears when she travels to cold countries. It's become so much me that finding it would be like finding me. So it's got to be a diary in hiding.

When I write in it, I feel as if I've got a set of wings, and I'm flying over my life and looking down and thinking, Anita, it's not as bad as you think.

July 2, 1961, Sunday afternoon

Another dreary Sunday, worrying about Papi. It's been over a month since I saw him. Sometimes I find myself forgetting what he even looks like, and then I feel bad, like my forgetfulness means he is gone forever.

When I get this way, I don't care about following my schedule or writing in my diary or daydreaming about Oscar. All I want to do is lie on my mat in the closet. Mami gets upset with me.

Come on, Anita, she scolds. You can't lie around all day. Who do you think you are, the Queen of Sheba?

Queen of the Walk-in Closet is more like it.

July 3, 1961, Monday night

The little Marías gave us such a scare this afternoon. Tía Mari was out doing grocery shopping at Wimpy's, and she must have thought she locked up her bedroom door as usual, but she hadn't. Mami and I were in the walk-in closet, with the door open for some ventilation and light, playing concentration, being quiet but not especially careful, when suddenly we heard the little girls coming into the bedroom.

Mami's going to be mad, one of them was saying—I couldn't tell which one.

She is not! said another. She won't even know.

Then there were sounds of opening drawers, and giggles, and one of them saying, you put on too much. They were at the vanity, trying on the lipsticks and perfumes, which I've done in my own mami's bedroom countless times.

Look what you did! You spilled it.

Then one of them said, Let's go see Mami's bear, which is the way they refer to their mother's fur coat hanging in this closet.

Mami and I froze. Our concentration game was spread out on the floor. We had no time to pick it up or cross over to the bathroom closets, so we just backed in among the clothes.

Suddenly, we heard someone else coming into the room. What are you girls doing? You know you're not supposed to be in here. It was Oscar! I hadn't heard his voice in so long. It sounded deeper, more like a man's voice than a boy's.

The little girls scrambled off, but curious Oscar stayed on, looking around. Soon the steps came around the corner and into the narrow hall, and then Oscar stepped inside the closet and ran his hand over the hanging suits and dresses, then stopped cold. Something had caught his eye. Very quietly, he backed out of the closet and shut the door.

Mami and I stayed hidden until we heard Tía Mari coming back. Virgen María! she cried. I believe I left the door unlocked.

On the floor of the closet, our concentration game was undisturbed—all the center cards facedown. But one card had been turned over: the queen of hearts!

July 4, 1961, Tuesday early morning

Before breakfast, I heard a little pebble strike the window of the bathroom. Then another. I didn't dare look out just in case. But when a third went ping!, curiosity got the better of me, and I peeked out the high window—

Oscar was standing in the yard, looking up. I ducked down before he saw me.

Later

I've been wondering if Oscar did see me?

So just now, I took the queen of hearts, slipped it out the window, and watched it sailing down to the yard below.

July 5, 1961, Wednesday, after siesta

Yesterday being the day of independence for the United States, Wimpy had a barbecue behind his store. The Mancinis were invited. Tío Pepe says that Wimpy knows where we are and is doing all he can to ensure our safety, whatever that means.

Was Chucha there? I asked Tía Mari.

Was she there! She and Oscar would not stop talking.

I touched the spot on my cheek, trying to calm myself down. But *my imagination has been going wild. Could they have been talking about . . . me?*

Oscar was again outside early this morning, looking up!

July 6, 1961, *Thursday evening news*

This evening, a surprise: Tía Mari brought me The Arabian Nights, which has to be one of my all-time favorite storybooks. When she saw the smile on my face, she said, So he was right.

It turns out Tía Mari asked Oscar this morning what book he might recommend for someone about his age, and he pulled this one out.

I opened the book, and there it was as a bookmark—the queen of hearts!

July 7, 1961, *Friday night*

Just knowing that I might have a secret communication going with Oscar makes every day brighter. I'm spending a lot more time in the bathroom, trying out hairstyles.

This afternoon, Mami saw me fussing and said, Who's going to see you here, for heaven's sake, Anita?

My face burned. Of course, she's right. But still, I told her what Tío Pepe had said about the Marquis de Sade. Mami just answered with one of Chucha's sayings: Dress the monkey in silk, he's still a monkey!

During supper tonight, Tío Pepe got into a long explanation about how human beings aren't using their full potential. If the brain were this plate, he said, we're using this grain of rice. Einstein maybe used this wedge of avocado. Galileo, this yuca patty.

(To think how much potential I'm wasting combing my hair and wondering if I'm pretty enough!)

How do you know when you're using your full potential? I asked Tío Pepe. But before he could get a word out, Tía Mari said, I'll tell you

127

when you're using your full brain power—when you're smart enough to eat your supper before it gets cold. That made even Tío Pepe smile and dig in.

July 8, 1961, *Saturday evening*

Reading The Arabian Nights *again has started me thinking . . . can stuff like this really happen? A girl who saves her life by telling a cruel sultan a bunch of stories? Let's say El Jefe had taken me away to his big bedroom, like he wanted to do with Lucinda. Could I have told him some stories that would have changed his evil heart? Or are some people so awful that nothing can really get inside them and make a difference?*

I asked Tío Pepe, and he said that is the million-dollar question. He said many great thinkers like Knee-chi (sp??) and Hide-digger (sp???) tried but never came up with a satisfactory answer (and they were working with a lot bigger plate of brains than I am).

Tía Mari has promised to ask Oscar for another book recommendation.

July 9, 1961, *Sunday, late afternoon*

Mami and I have been alone all day, as the Mancinis went to the beach to visit friends. They shut up the house and sent all the servants away. The place is so creepy and quiet. And of course, every little noise scares us.

Mami and I played cards for a while, and then we went into the bathroom, and Mami herself put my hair up in a bun like a ballerina and made me up with a little lipstick and rouge.

Mami, I asked as we studied the results in the mirror, do you think I look just the tiniest bit like Audrey Hepburn?

Much prettier, Mami said.

She couldn't have said anything nicer! I forgave her all her nerve attacks and how she hasn't said one nice thing to me in ages. I turned around and gave her a bone-crunching hug.

Watch you don't break something, Mami said, laughing, I can't exactly go to the doctor's right now.

Later, Sunday night

Tía Mari came back from the beach with some seashells Oscar and the little girls collected.

I picked one to take with me to the closet, a shiny spiral with brown freckles. But then I remembered how Chucha used to say girls who keep seashells die old maids, and I took it back to Tía Mari and said, Keep this for me until I'm married.

She looked a little surprised.

Tío Pepe just returned from the embassy next door with some exciting news—Mundín is going to be evacuated soon! It seems there is an Italian cruise ship in the harbor headed for Miami. The ambassador was hoping to get us all on board, but the captain said he could only take one mysterious passenger, as more would be too high a risk in view of how the SIM are carefully monitoring all ports of exit.

Mami is worried about Mundín and whether the transfer will go okay, and that starts her worrying about Papi and Tío Toni. She isn't sleeping as well anymore, as she doesn't have any Equanil left. Tía Mari says that the drugstores are all out. It seems the whole country is taking tranquilizers.

July 11, 1961, Tuesday night

Last night, as we lay on our mats in the closet, Mami started telling me stories about growing up on a sugar estate where her father was the resident doctor. It was like old times again, when we used to get along so well.

129

The best story was about when she turned fifteen, and her parents threw her a big quinceañera party. She wore a long white dress like a bride's and a tiara of sugar flowers made especially for her by the plantation pastry cook.

When the party was over, Mami really wanted to save that crown, but her little brother Edilberto found that sweet crown and sucked off the sugar rosettes. All that was left was the wire frame!

You laugh now, Mami laughed, but I cried as if he'd eaten up my heart.

Speaking of queens, Mami said, I don't know if you remember how six years ago, El Jefe's daughter was crowned Queen Angelita I? You were just a little girl, but when you saw her in the papers wearing that ridiculous silk gown that cost 80,000 dollars, you said, Mami, is that our queen? And I didn't know what to say because the help was all around, and so I said, we don't actually have a royal family here, but Angelita was made into a queen by her father. And for a while afterward when we asked you what you wanted for your birthday or for Christmas or Vieja Belén or Los Tres Reyes Magos, you'd say you wanted your father to make you a queen.

And so for your next birthday, you remember? Your father made you a marshmallow crown. You wore that thing all day long in the sun, you wouldn't take it off, and those soft marshmallows began to melt on your hair. We had a time washing them out.

The thought of Papi made us both fall silent. I lay in the dark, remembering Papi and Tío Toni, walking on the beach with me, and the sand and the wind, and Tío Toni joking, Let's throw her in, and Papi holding on tight and laughing—

I reached out for Mami's hand just as she was reaching out for mine.

July 12, 1961, Wednesday night

Wimpy and Mr. Washburn have been trying to do all they can. But Papi's name and Tío Toni's were not listed among those of the prisoners the OAS interviewed when they came. I don't need Mami to tell me that's not a good sign.

I heard some of the stories the prisoners told during those interviews. Mami and the Mancinis were listening to the OAS report on Radio Swan tonight. They thought I was writing in my diary in the bathroom, but I was still in the hallway. The announcer read out passages, his voice matter-of-fact, but the facts themselves were horrible.

Prisoners complained about how their fingernails were pulled out, their eyes sewn open. About being put on an electric chair called the Throne and given shocks so they would tell who else was involved. About how one of them was fed a steak, only to find out it was the flesh of his own son.

For the first time in a long time, I slipped my little crucifix in my mouth and said an Our Father. Then I went in the bathroom and threw up my supper.

July 13, 1961, Thursday night

What a surprise!

We were out in the bedroom with the Mancinis, listening to the news, when there was a knock: the maid announcing that the Mancinis had visitors.

Who is it? Tía Mari asked through the locked door.

El embajador with a lady, the maid replied.

Tía Mari and Tío Pepe were not expecting the ambassador, and so of course they suspected a SIM trick. We instantly went into emergency procedure.

A little later, we heard Tía Mari coming back into the bedroom with *someone else. We heard her locking the bedroom door. Then she came into the bathroom and said, it's okay. You can come out now.*

So we crept out of the crawl-space closets, thinking the other person was Tío Pepe or the ambassador himself, but as Mami and I headed out, there was a blond girl sitting on Tía Mari's bed with her back to us.

We hurried back to the bathroom.

But Tía Mari called, come on out here, somebody wants to see you.

Mami and I were shocked. We all know that we are not to show our faces to anyone, except our two hosts.

Tía Mari appeared at the door of the bathroom with this blond girl wearing sunglasses and a dress that you could tell she didn't much like by the way she was looking down, disgusted at herself. Then she glanced up with the most familiar eyes in the world.

Mundín! Mami cried out.

Hush! Tía Mari said, laughing. So it works, she said. I told el embajador that the best test would be if his own mother and sister didn't recognize him.

Mundín was on his way to the boat. He hugged us good-bye. I'm not all that happy about this, he said, and I don't mean the disguise. I mean leaving you. Papi always said if anything should happen—

He stopped when Mami started to cry.

Tía Mari let me walk with Mundín to the door of the bedroom. With every step, I felt my heart falling apart, like that torture I heard about on the radio where a man was slowly cut up alive.

Mundín turned to me, and they say boys don't cry, so maybe it was because he was dressed as a girl, but there were tears in my big brother's eyes.

As for me, I was sobbing so hard, I could barely breathe.

July 15, 1961, *Saturday morning*

Mami and I stayed up late last night talking. Earlier, we had been listening to Radio Swan, and the announcer closed the program by saying, ¡Que Vivan Las Mariposas! Long Live the Butterflies!

That must have got Mami thinking about Papi because she started talking about the old days and how Papi and my uncles became involved in the underground movement against the dictator.

After your father came back from college in the States, Mami explained, he got so busy working and raising his own family that he didn't pay much attention to politics. Mami was whispering real low, so as not to disturb the Mancinis. I had to roll to the very edge of my mat to hear her.

But things began to go from bad to worse. Our friends were disappearing. One of your uncles was arrested. But we didn't know what to do.

Then we heard about these sisters who were organizing a movement to bring freedom to the country. Everyone called them Las Mariposas, the Butterflies, because they had put wings on all our hearts.

Some of your uncles, like Tío Carlos and Tío Toni, joined right away, Mami went on. But Papi held back, afraid to risk all our lives.

Somehow, the SIM found out about the movement. They started arresting people, and their families, torturing them, and getting more and more names. Mamita and Papito and your uncles got out while they could. Tío Carlos made it just in time.

As for the Butterflies, they were ambushed and murdered on a lonely mountain road, their car thrown over a cliff to make it all look like an accident.

And it was then that your father and I took up the torch of the Butterflies and began the struggle again.

I couldn't believe my own mother with her bad nerves was part of a secret plot! But suddenly, like one of those lamps you click one more turn and it throws an even brighter light, I saw her at Papi's old Remington, typing up declarations, or out in the yard, burning incriminating stuff, or in the garden shed, covering a sack of guns with an old tarp. My Joan-of-Arc mother, my Butterfly mami! I felt so proud of her!

Mami went on telling about how the movement spread all over the country. Everyone was joining up. Papi contacted Wimpy and Mr. Farland, whom he knew from his college days, and the Americans agreed to help them. Some other men even persuaded General Pupo to join the plot. The General said that once he had proof that El Jefe was out of the way, he, Pupo, would take control of the government and hold free elections.

But then, things started to fall apart, Mami said. She sounded like one of those wind-up toys winding down. Washington got cold feet. The night of the ajusticiamiento, no one could find Pupo. The SIM moved in fast.

The end, Mami finished. Her voice was barely a whisper.

I closed my eyes, remembering the promise Papi wanted me to make, and I thought, No, Mami, not the end. Long live the Butterflies!

July 17, 1961, Monday, late night

As we were getting ready for bed tonight, Tía Mari said, Oh yes, I almost forgot. Chucha came up to me at Wimpy's today and said something I didn't quite understand. All three of us were in the bathroom, brushing our teeth. We have to do all our noise simultaneously.

She said to tell you to get ready to use your wings again.

Mami looked surprised. I thought no one but you and Wimpy knew we were here.

Believe me, Tía Mari said, I didn't let on. But she followed me all through the store and then out to the car. And again, she said the same *thing. I said, Chucha, I don't know what you're talking about. And she just gave me that look of hers and then she took this out of her pocket.*

It was a holy card of San Miguel lifting his huge wings above the slain dragon.

My heart has a pair of wings, too—one wing fluttering with excitement because maybe we'll soon be free! The other shaking with fear because I don't really want to be free without Papi and Tío Toni.

July 18, 1961, *Tuesday night*

I'm using my little flashlight Tía Mari gave me, as the electricity is out again all over the capital today. Tío Pepe's theory is that it's a SIM sabotage, one more reason to roll out the army tanks.

We are all feeling very hopeful, as there is a rally planned for tomorrow. There was also a letter that took up a whole page in the paper, stating the rights of man, and signed with a lot of important people's names.

Tío Pepe says this is our Magna Carta, and I'm so glad I was paying attention that day in history class so I don't have to ask what that is.

July 19, 1961, *Wednesday—we can hear the rally going on, shouts of* LIBERTAD!

There is a very small chance, very small, Tío Pepe says, holding his thumb and forefinger so close they almost seem to be touching, that we might be able to get on a private flight that will be taking a bunch of Americans to Florida. Wimpy has been trying to work it so that Mami and I can board that plane at the last minute.

Suddenly, the thought of leaving our hideaway is scary.

Tío Pepe once told me about this experiment with monkeys who were caged for so long that when the doors were left open, they wouldn't come out.

I wonder what it will be like to be free? Not to need wings because you don't need to fly away from your country?

July 20, 1961, *Thursday*

Oscar and I have a secret language of books going. So far, he has picked out El Pequeño Príncipe, Poesías de José Martí, Cuentos de Shakespeare para Niños, The Swiss Family Robinson. When I'm done with each book, I give it back to Tía Mari with the queen of hearts card back in it.

Then, when the next book arrives, sure enough, there's the queen of hearts bookmark!

What will become of Oscar and me? I wonder if there'll be a movie about us, like Romeo and Juliet? I just hope and pray our story has a happier ending!

July 28, 1961, *Friday, another rally on the street*

Because of all these rallies, the SIM have started arresting people again and conducting their house-to-house searches.

We are on the alert from Wimpy that our evacuation might be sooner rather than later. The problem is how to move us to an undisclosed location where we can take a flight to freedom.

The Mancinis are trying to figure something out.

There have been no more book deliveries. On Monday, Tía Mari sent the girls and Oscar and Doña Margot away to their friends with the beach house. Because of the rallies, there's lots of gunfire and massive arrests. Several bullets came through our old classroom window that faces the street. Thank goodness the children were already out of the house. Tía Mari refuses to go in there.

Mami and I are getting on each other's nerves again with all the tension. I try to do my pacing where she isn't doing hers, but there's not much room inside a closet.

It's hard to concentrate on anything, even writing in my diary. I haven't had the energy to keep to my schedule.

Tía Mari suggests we entertain ourselves playing cards, but when Mami sorts through the deck, she says, What on earth happened to the queen of hearts?

July 30, 1961, *Sunday—most BORING day so far!*

This morning, the Mancinis drove out to the beach for the day to see the kids, so it has been like a tomb around here. All I've done is read and nap and look at magazines and eat the leftover waterbreads from break-fast, and now I'm going to try to write—

We're in the crawl space— and I'm scribbling down this note by flashlight just in case anyone finds this diary—

—There was a huge roar in the backyard like a plane landing—now a crashing sound at the downstairs door—

Oh my god—they're coming through the house!!!!

My hand is shaking so hard—but I want to leave this record just so the world knows—

ten

Freedom Cry

"Anita, *por favor*," Mami calls from the other room. "Turn that thing off."

I'm sitting in front of the television at the Hotel Beverly, where my grandparents have been renting an apartment on the top floor. We've been in New York City already over a month and a half. I mark off every day on the calendar. Today, I made such a heavy **x** that I tore through the paper. September 18, 1961, isn't even over, but it's already gone!

The days are getting cooler. Down on the street, ten flights below, the little toy trees are beginning to turn reddish, like someone is lighting a match to them.

Every time I get a chance, I watch TV. I tell Mami that I want to learn more about this country. But really, I just want to keep my mind off everything I could be worrying about right now.

Like the phone call Mami is about to make from the other room. Twice a week, she calls Mr. Washburn in Washington to find out if there's any news about Papi and my uncle. We all sit around— my grandparents, Mamita and Papito, Lucinda and Mundín and me—watching the reactions on her face.

"With Mr. Washburn, *por favor*," I hear Mami saying. I go up to the television to turn it off, and just then, she comes on, the only Spanish lady I've ever seen on TV. There's also a Cuban guy called Ricky Ricardo, who has a wacky American wife who reminds me of Mrs. Washburn. This lady carries a big basket of bananas on her head like the *marchantas* in the market calling out their wares.

I turn down the volume and sing along under my breath.

The first time I saw her, I couldn't believe what she was saying: *"I'm Anita Banana and I'm here to stay."*

"NO!" I screamed at the TV and clapped my hands over my ears. "I am not staying, I am not staying!"

Lucinda ran into the room. *"¿Qué pasa?* What on earth are you screaming about, Anita?" Thank goodness Mami and Mamita and Papito were out with Mundín, getting him a winter jacket, otherwise my screaming would have shot their fragile nerves. "You want us to get thrown out of here?"

I nodded and then shook my head. Of course I didn't want to get thrown out and sent back to live in a closet. But I wanted the dictatorship to be over so we could go home to live as a family again. "The lady," I said, pointing to the silent screen.

"What about her?" Lucinda asked, turning the volume back up. She watched the rest of the commercial. "You're crying about her?"

"No, not about her, about what she said." I explained the lady's prediction as if the television were a crystal ball.

Lucinda let out one of her long-suffering sighs. "Ay, Anita, that's not what she's saying." Lucinda swirled her hips, imitating the lady. "She's saying Chiquita Banana, not Anita Banana and she's here to say, not stay!"

I guess my nerves were pretty shot, too.

I'm still seeing ghosts and signs everywhere. And Chucha isn't around to help me interpret them.

"I am so sorry to be molesting you, Mr. Washburn," Mami is saying as I come in the room. Lucinda has explained to her that *molestar* does not mean *bother* in English as it does in Spanish. But Mami says how is she supposed to remember all the crazy ways the Americans have changed Spanish around. Sometimes, sad as I am, even I have to smile at Mami.

"Yes, yes, I understand, yes, Mr. Washburn," Mami is saying. With each *yes*, I can hear her voice getting weaker. Her knuckles are bone-white from holding the receiver so tight. "No news *is* good news. You are right. We are so much in gratitude to you," she says at the end.

"Nothing," Mami says quietly after she hangs up. "They're trying to put pressure on Trujillo Junior to leave the country. Then the prisoners will be released. We just have to keep hoping and praying," she adds more cheerfully. She doesn't sound very convinced.

"*¡Exactamente!*" my grandfather agrees, trying to inject confidence into all of us. But my grandmother begins weeping. "*Mis pobres hijos, mi pobre país.*" Her poor sons, her poor country!

Lucinda joins in, and before long, Mami and I are also crying. Mundín hurries off to the bathroom, where I'm sure he cries, too.

My grandfather puts on his overcoat and heads for the drugstore to get my grandmother some more of her blood-pressure medicine.

I want to go with him, but I can't because it's sort of illegal that we're staying in their rooms with them, as they would have to pay more. Papito has told the doorman who's Puerto Rican that ours is "a temporary situation," and the doorman says he understands, just to be *discretos*. So we try to be discreet and go out one by one, so it doesn't look like we know each other but are just separate people staying in the hotel rooms on the lower floors.

I go stand by the window and watch for Papito to come out downstairs, an old man in a Panama hat—one of the few familiar faces in this country where the only people we know are the ones who came with us.

The day we were surprised in our hiding place, I had no idea that it would be my good-bye to my country. I actually thought the SIM had discovered us and it was good-bye to my life.

That's why, scared as I was, I kept writing in my diary. I wanted someone to know what had happened to us.

But when the crawl-space doors were thrown open, it was Wimpy and his paratroopers coming to the rescue! The Mancinis, who were away at the beach, didn't even know that the airlift would be that day. A number of things had to fall in place for our evacuation, and that Sunday, July 30, they came together at the last minute.

I had been about to stash away my diary under a loose board. But Wimpy grabbed me and picked me up, and the diary came away with me in my hand. An unmarked helicopter was waiting on the embassy grounds to airlift us out, and there wasn't a minute to spare. Outside on the streets, an angry rally was going on, and the SIM were too busy with crowd control to notice a dragonfly helicopter flying by with a terrified mother and daughter inside.

North of the city, we landed on an abandoned airstrip, where a cargo plane was waiting. A van drove up with some other people, some of whom I recognized. Wimpy helped everyone climb on board, a grim look on his face, his eagle tattoo pumping away. As our plane took off, I glanced out the window at the cracked tarmac and the swaying palms waving good-bye, and I thought I saw a flash of purple getting back into the van with Wimpy.

We flew higher and higher, over green valleys and dark, ridged mountains, and then over the coast, waves breaking on the white sands. Miles below, Oscar was in one of those tiny beach houses . . . maybe looking up! How long before he returned home? Would he realize right away that I was no longer hidden in his parents' closet, using his queen of hearts to mark my place in *The Swiss Family Robinson?*

So many people and places I might not ever get to see again! Looking down, I saw a quilt of faces and memories spreading out over the sea—Monsito carrying our sack of *plátanos* in his wheelbarrow, Tío Pepe with his white socks, Porfirio watering the ginger plants while singing his sad songs—and the purple thread stitching piece to piece was Chucha, my dear Chucha, who had helped me survive this year of my life falling apart!

I stared out the window, too shocked even to cry, until we climbed into the clouds and there was nothing else to see. A little while later, I leaned against Mami and fell asleep.

When she shook me awake, it was dark outside the plane. We had landed. Somehow, I stumbled in my half-sleep across a runway, Mami holding on to me, to a bigger airplane taking us to New York City.

The next I knew, I was looking down at the view I had seen on the postcards Lucinda used to send us that left even Chucha speechless—buildings so tall that I couldn't quite believe they were real, and patches of green like scatter rugs, and tiny antlike people whom I could blot out just by putting my hand on the small square of the window. How could I live in this world full of strangers and gray light instead of a country of cousins and family and family friends and year-round sunshine?

We landed and entered a terminal where officials took us into a room to issue us special papers. Then one of them shook our hands and said, "Welcome to the United States of America," and pointed us out of Immigration. And there was my answer to how I would survive in this strange, new world: My family was waiting for us— Mundín and Lucinda, my grandparents, Carla, her sisters, and Tía Laura and Tío Carlos and Tía Mimí—all of them calling out, "Anita! Carmen!" Carla says my face was worth a thousand bucks as the family rushed forward and locked us in their arms.

By the end of September, we still have no news of Papi and Tío Toni. The Garcías have invited us to move out to their house in Queens, but Mami won't hear of it. Any day now, we will be returning home. The *campo* suburbs are for those who have decided to settle down in the United States, like the Garcías. New York City is where you stay on your way back to where you came from.

While we are waiting around, Mami decides that we should learn perfect English. Lucinda already is a pro from being here since February, but Mundín and I could use practice. "Papi will be so pleased!" she says excitedly. There is an uneasy silence when she says these things. But I so want to believe her that I'll do anything, *anything* that might help make this happen.

Mami goes to a nearby Catholic school and asks the principal if we can sit in on any class till we go back home. The principal is a nun with a bonnet like a baby doll, except it's black. She is a Sister of Charity, and maybe that is why she is so kind and says yes, she will put us wherever there is a spot.

The next day, I don't think she is so kind. I am sitting at a small desk in the second grade, the only elementary classroom that had extra space. The teacher, Sister Mary Joseph, has a sweet face with pale whiskers and watery blue eyes as if she is always in tears. Her breath is musty, like an old suitcase that hasn't been opened in years.

"Annie is a very special student," she tells the class, "a refugee from a dictatorship." When she says this, I stare down at the wooden floor and try not to cry.

"She came here with her family in order to be free," Sister Mary Joseph is explaining. But my family is not all here, I feel like saying. And how can I be free when my mind is all worried about Papi and my whole self is so sad, I can barely get up some mornings?

"Would you like to tell the class a little something about the Dominican Republic?" the old nun prompts me.

Where do I begin telling strangers about a place whose smell is on my skin and whose memory is always in my head? To them, it's just a geography lesson; to me, it's home. Besides, talking about my country would make me too sad right now. I stand in front of this roomful of staring little kids, not saying a single word. At the very least I should show them that I can speak their language, so they don't think I'm a complete moron who is almost thirteen and still in the second grade.

"Thank you," I murmur, "for letting me into your country."

Sister Mary Joseph gives me an assignment to do on my own. I am to write a composition about what I remember from my native country.

"Maybe it'll be easier to write down memories rather than just think on your feet," she suggests. She shows me how I'm supposed to make a little cross at the top of each page, and then print the initials *J.M.J.*, dedicating my work to Jesus, Mary, and Joseph.

Below, on the first line, I am to put my own name, which she writes out as *Annie Torres*, and the date, October 4, 1961.

I bend to my work, make my little cross on top of a clean page, dedicating my composition to J.M.J. But then, I add M.T. & A.T., Mundo and Antonio de la Torre.

"What's that?" Sister Mary Joseph says, peering over my shoulder.

"My father and my uncle." I point to each set of initials.

She is about to protest, but then her watery blue eyes get even more watery. "I am so sorry," she whispers—as if Papi and Tío Toni are dead!

"I will be seeing them soon," I explain.

"Of course you will, dear," Sister Mary Joseph says, nodding. Today, her breath smells like the sachets my grandmother sticks in her underwear drawer.

As the class goes over cursive letters, I work on my assignment. At first I can't think of what to say, but then I pretend I'm writing in my diary again. Soon I'm filling page after page, making lists of people and foods and places I miss, describing them using metaphors like Mrs. Brown taught us. I also write down my favorites of Chucha's sayings:

> *With patience and calm, even a burro can climb a palm.*
> *Dress the monkey in silk, he's still a monkey.*
> *You can't dry yesterday's laundry with tomorrow's sun.*

As I write, I can almost hear Chucha at my side whispering, *"Fly! Fly free!"* Those were the last words she ever spoke to me. But how can I be really free without Papi in my life? If something happens to him, then the part that is the wings in me would die.

When I hand in my composition, Sister Mary Joseph reads it over, marking pencil in hand. I stand by her big desk, watching her pencil dip down, correcting my mistakes. She chuckles when she gets to the page with Chucha's sayings.

"Very good," she remarks, although the pages are full of little red marks.

By the end of October, Papi is still in prison and Trujillo Junior is still in power. He is getting crazier with revenge and refuses to cooperate with the Americans, so even Mr. Washburn doesn't have a whole lot of details. I decide to write to Oscar, who always seemed to know about everything, and ask him what he knows.

I've tried writing him before. But every time I sat down, I felt a wave of homesickness, and I had to put the letter away.

But this time, I have a mission, though I've got to be extra careful on account of the censors. I start out telling him all about *Nueva York*; how cold it's gotten and how uncomfortable it is to wear so many heavy clothes; how the people don't smile a whole lot, so you can't really tell if they like you or not; how I am in school learning lots of English (I leave out the part about second grade); how my teacher, Sister Mary Joseph, is making me write down stories like the girl in *The Arabian Nights*; how she did a whole geography segment on the island, and Mami fried *pastelitos* for me to take in, which everyone liked a lot. I mix in the good and the bad and sometimes, I admit, when there's not much good to report, I make some things up.

Then, very casually, I slip in, *"How are things in the sultan's court?"* I underline *sultan's*, but then I erase my underlining, in case it is too obvious a clue.

I give the letter to my grandfather to mail because I don't really want Mami to know I'm writing to a boy, even if he is my cousin. But Papito looks at the address on the envelope and explains that no mail is getting through. The country is all closed up, just like this place called Berlin, where an iron curtain has come down that keeps people from going in or getting out.

I take the letter back and tear it up in lots of little pieces. Then I open the window and watch them fall, a sprinkle of white to the ground below. Some of the people on the street look up. Maybe they think it's snowing? The García girls out in Queens have told me all about winter in this country. By Christmas, they've promised, I'll get to see the snow.

"I won't be here by then," I keep telling them.

But as each day goes by, and the leaves all fall off like the trees have some disease, and October turns into November, I wonder if I'm going to be here for a lot longer than just the first snowfall of this year.

Often, on the way home from school, I'll stop at the grocery store for a visit. No matter how sad I am, every time I step in front of the door and it opens by itself, I feel a rush of excitement like I'm back at Wimpy's. I love to walk down the aisles, half expecting I'll find Chucha with the big feather duster the stock boy uses to clean the shelves. I can't believe all the boxes and brands. Soups and sauces, cans of this and cans of that, a dozen different cereals, tons of candies. Even the animals in this country get lots of choices. Six kinds of cat food! What would Monsito say about that?!

Today, I don't know what gets into me, but instead of just looking, I decide to take a cart. I go up and down each aisle, filling the basket with things I really like, pretending I have the money to buy them. When I'm done with all the aisles, the basket is piled so high, I can barely see over it. I head back the way I came, carefully putting everything back in its place.

Suddenly, a big, chesty man is barreling down the aisle toward me. He wears a white apron like a butcher and his face looks like a raw piece of meat, pinkish and maybe angry. I can't tell for sure with American faces what they are feeling, but I would say this man looks angry.

I try to act like I'm old enough to be grocery-shopping by myself. In a month, I'll be turning thirteen. Last week, a lady in the elevator at the hotel guessed I was fourteen! My baby face is sinking down to the past and a new face is coming to the surface, with my grandmother's slightly turned-up nose and my father's deep-set eyes and my mother's coffee-with-milk-color skin. I guess the only thing that is all mine is the scar above my left eye, where Mundín once hit me with a pellet from a BB gun he had aimed at the sky.

The man stops directly in front of my cart like a roadblock. "Do you have the money to buy all this, young lady?" His tone of voice suggests that he knows I don't.

I make the mistake of looking into his glaring eyes. In their harsh light, I am sure it shows that I am not one hundred percent certain I should be doing what I am doing. I stammer out a barely audible, "Sí, señor," too scared at the moment to be able to speak in a second language.

"Don't you understand English?" he says, taking hold of my arm.

I'm about to tell him I do, but already he is yanking me to the front of the store and out the opening door to the sidewalk. Some people walking by turn their heads to look.

"I don't want you coming back without an adult, you hear me?" He is patting me all up and down checking to see if I've taken something.

At first, I just stand there, ashamed, submitting to his search as if I've done something wrong. But when he slaps his big hand on my chest, I cry out, "I wasn't doing anything! This is a free country!" Actually, I'm not really sure this is true. Maybe this is a free country only for Americans? Maybe if a policeman happens by, my whole family will be deported home, where we'll all be killed by the dictator's son?

This thought is so terrifying that it's as if I have Superman strength. I wrench myself free from the man's grasp and take off running down the block, turning left, then right, trying to lose anyone who might be following me to the Beverly. When I get to the hotel, I rush past the American doorman, who is not as friendly as the Puerto Rican, and around the revolving door into the lobby, where, rather than wait for the elevator, I race up the stairs two at a time to the tenth floor, my heart pounding so hard, I'm sure it's going to explode.

I stop before our door, trying to catch my breath and calm the wild panic that I'm sure shows on my face. Inside, I hear my grandmother crying. Mami has probably just finished one of her twice-a-week calls to Mr. Washburn in Washington.

Part of me wants to avoid going in and facing even more sad news. But the terror of deportation is bigger than a disappointment I'm becoming used to. So, I knock very lightly, and call out in a little voice, "Soy yo." It's just me.

Mundín opens the door, his face so drained and pale that I'm sure the police have somehow tracked me down and my family is in deep trouble.

I start crying. "I wasn't doing anything wrong."

Mundín takes my hand. "Mr. Washburn is here," he says in a flat voice, like a bulldozer has just run over it.

As I follow my brother into the main room, I'm puzzling over how Mr. Washburn could have gotten here all the way from Washington to deport us when the grocery store incident just happened? Maybe he was already in New York? Maybe the grocery store man had planned an ambush beforehand with the State Department? But even as I entertain these farfetched possibilities, I know that I'm just trying *not* to think of the obvious reason Mr. Washburn would be here, a reason more horrible than any angry store manager or policeman coming to report me for getting into trouble.

On the couch where Mundín sleeps at night sit Mami and Lucinda holding on to each other. My grandfather is leaning forward on the recliner, listening to something Mr. Washburn is saying. Another man in a military uniform with his back to me is standing behind Mr. Washburn's chair. In the other room, I hear my grandmother crying. "She had to go lie down," Mundín explains. "She had to take a tranquilizer pill."

"Why?" I ask. My heart is tottering on the edge of a very high place, and I am waiting, breathlessly, for it to either fall down into a thousand pieces or be rescued by good news at the last minute.

Mr. Washburn stands up and folds his arms around me. When he lets go, I follow Mundín to a place on the couch beside Papito's recliner, my hand on my chest as if I could reach in and steady my heart inside my ribs. As I go by Mami, she looks up and starts crying.

My grandfather reaches over and takes my two hands in his. "We are all going to have to be very brave," he says quietly. His eyes are also red. Then he says the words I will never forget. "Your father and uncle are dead."

"We got a report yesterday," Mr. Washburn begins explaining. "The dictator's family had agreed to leave." His voice is official-sounding, but every once in a while, little clouds of sadness travel across it.

"Just before dawn, the son took off for his beach estate. Meanwhile, his SIM buddies drove over to the prison and seized the six remaining conspirators and took them to the beach—" Mr. Washburn stops abruptly.

After a moment, he adds, *"Lo siento,"* which means much more than that he is sorry, but that he feels what we are feeling.

"Tell us!" Mami orders. "I want to know how they died. I want my children to hear this. I want my country to hear this. I want the United States to hear this."

She sounds so absolutely sure, Mr. Washburn clears his throat and goes on. "Trujillo Junior and his cronies were quite drunk. We're not sure, but they might also have been drugged up. At any rate, they tied the prisoners to palm trees and shot them, one by one, until they were all dead. Then the bodies were taken out to sea and dumped over the side of the boat."

Before Mr. Washburn is even finished, Mami is sobbing, great gouging sobs, as if she is trying to scoop out all the sadness inside herself so there will be room for other feelings. Lucinda sobs, too, but in a distracted way, watching Mami, afraid of such huge grief none of us has ever seen before. Papito and Mundín dab at their eyes, my grandfather with his monogrammed handkerchief that reminds me of Papi's, Mundín with the back of his hand.

But I don't cry. Not right away. I listen carefully until the very end. I want to be with Papi and Tío Toni every step of the way.

When Mr. Washburn is done, Mami and Mundín and Lucinda and I stand up and put our arms around each other. Papito joins us, all of us crying into the empty space at the center of our family.

eleven

Snow Butterflies

"What is it going to look like?" I ask my cousin Carla.

"It's hard to describe," Carla says. "Just wait and see."

We are staying with the Garcías in Queens until we find our own place nearby. Mami and Lucinda and Mundín are inside with the rest of the cousins and my aunts and uncles and grandparents, but Carla and her sisters are standing with me in their backyard in mittens and hats and coats, waiting for my first snow to fall. All day the radio has been predicting a white Thanksgiving. The gray sky looks heavy and low, a piñata filled with snow.

Carla has grown up a lot since last year when we were best friends back home. She wears her hair in a flip with a hairband instead of tucking it behind her ears and puts glossy stuff on her lips, so they don't chap, she says, but it looks sort of like lipstick. She speaks English so fast that sometimes I have to stop her and say, *"Por favor en español,"* which Tía Laura loves to hear, as she worries that the girls are forgetting their native language from having to speak only English in school.

"Usually, it doesn't snow this early," Carla is saying. She talks as though she's lived in the United States all her life! "This is special, Anita."

"It brings good luck if it snows before Christmas," Yo adds.

"You're making that up!" Carla cuts her eyes at her younger sister. And maybe Yo is inventing things again. But I think it's sweet how the Garcías are trying to make it up to me after what happened to Papi.

"Girls," Tía Laura calls from the kitchen window she's just opened. "We're almost ready to eat."

It's *el día del pavo,* as my grandparents call it, the day of the turkey, but I know from going to the American school that its real name is Thanksgiving, the day the Pilgrims in their black hats and capes gave thanks for surviving their first year in the United States. Some of my cousins have come down from the Bronx and my grandparents came from the city on a train that goes under the ground. We're not all here because Tío Fran and his family are in Miami, and Tía Mimí has a boyfriend, who's taken her over to meet his parents. But most . . . of the rest of our family is here.

Usually, Carla and her sisters have to help out, but today, there are too many cooks in the broth, as Tía Laura says. (Even I know that my aunt gets most of her sayings wrong in English.) So we've walked around the block I don't know how many times, past the house where a cute boy in Carla's class lives. Carla is always falling in love and talking about getting married. Mami says, and I agree, that Carla has become a little boy-crazy in this country. But Carla claims that that's what happens when a girl gets to seventh grade. (I hate to tell her, but it happened to me in sixth.)

We moved in with the Garcías a couple of weeks ago, after hearing the news. Right away, Mami registered me at the Catholic school Carla and her sisters are attending. I was put back in sixth grade because I'd missed most of it back home. But the principal, Sister Celeste, has promised that if I make progress, maybe I can be jumped up to Carla's grade by spring.

I had hoped we'd be long gone by then! But Mami now says

we're not going back, not for a long time, not till the wounds in our hearts have healed.

I wonder how long that'll be? How I'll ever get over the emptiness left behind by Papi?

Mami comes outside to tell us it's time to eat. She looks so sad and thin, wearing a black coat that belonged to Tía Laura that seems too big on her, even though she's the same size as my aunt, or used to be. Underneath the black coat is a black dress she's been wearing for weeks. She has little Fifi by the hand, who I guess was crying because she wanted to be outside with her three older sisters.

"Has it come yet?" Mami asks, looking up. Mami has seen snow before, when she traveled with Papi to the States one winter, but she's excited for me and keeps telling me about her first time. She and Papi scooped out balls from the windowsill of their hotel and threw them at each other inside the room. Since this morning, she's been checking the sky as if it were the turkey in the oven that might get overdone. But not a flake has fallen from the gray mistiness above. "I guess you better come in now," Mami says. "It might be a while, and you know how your mother gets." She eyes the García girls. They know. Tía Laura worries just about as much here as she used to back home.

We head inside, little Fifi running alongside her sisters. I'm trailing behind, but Mami waits up for me, then puts her arm around my waist. We've become close again in these last few months of hoping and praying that things would come out all right. Now that they haven't, she holds on to me whenever she gets the chance, as if she's afraid of losing me as well as everything else she's lost.

"How was your walk?" she asks me.

"It was okay," I say so she doesn't worry. But what can I report about the umpteenth time Carla has walked me by Kevin McLaughlin's house, hoping to catch a glimpse of him eating turkey inside?

"Hard to get used to everything so gray and dead." Mami sighs, glancing up at the bare trees. At the mention of death, I can feel her hand tighten on my waist. "Your first American Thanksgiving," she says, trying to sound cheerful. As I follow her indoors, I see out of the corner of my eye a little flake of dust, and then another. But no, I think, it couldn't be. I'm expecting lace doilies, like the ones my grandmother used to crochet before she had to leave her home behind and come to this country.

In the dining room, the big table is set with extra leaves to accommodate all the grown-ups. It looks like a gathering of blackbirds, everyone wearing black. I sit with *la juventud* at the smaller table set up for the kids by the picture window.

"We thank you, *Señor*, for these gifts," Tío Carlos begins, but he chokes up. Mundín says that our uncle has been feeling bad that he got out just in time, leaving my father and Tío Toni and others to bear the brunt of the dictator's son's wrath.

"Most of all, we thank you for bringing the family together," our grandfather picks up, "to mourn and to celebrate those who gave their lives for all of us."

"Amen!" Fifi calls out when nobody says anything. She's learning how to pray, and every time she knows a word, she yells it out, loud and clear. Everyone bursts out laughing, some of us through our tears.

* * *

Earlier today, Mrs. Washburn called Mami to say we were all in her thoughts this Thanksgiving. She spoke to Mami for a little bit and then Mami handed the phone to me.

"Hi," a familiar voice greeted me. "I'm sorry about your dad," Sam said. "My dad says he was a real hero."

I didn't know what to say. Only stupid things came to mind, like, "Thank you for saying you're sorry that my father was killed."

"So, do you like New York, Anita?"

I told him what I tell everyone who asks me. "It's okay." Sammy used to brag that this was the greatest country on earth. I hoped I wasn't offending him with my lackluster response.

"If you want to visit us, Mom says you and Lucinda and Mundín can come." By the way Sam was hesitating as he moved through that sentence, I could tell his mother was coaching him on the other end.

Carla was standing beside me, mouthing, "What?" I turned my face away so she'd stop. I had told her about Sammy, making him sound like an old boyfriend in order to keep up with my cousin's sophisticated life of seventh-grade romance.

"Thanks, Sam," I said when he finished his invitation. Even though we'd outgrown each other, Sam was kind of my first love, so I added, "We're getting our own place soon. Mami says when we do, I can have friends over. If you want to come here?"

"Wow! We could go to a Yankees game. Mom," he called out, "Anita just invited me to come to New York to see Yogi Berra and Mickey Mantle play."

I looked over at Carla, who was lifting her eyebrows at me curiously. I shook my head, just so she'd know. No, I did not want to grow up and marry Sam Washburn.

* * *

I'm so stuffed, I can't even finish what's on my plate. As soon as the tables are cleared, Yo starts asking if we can go out. Mami calls, "*Un segundito,*" from the kitchen, and in a moment, she comes back in, carrying a birthday cake in the shape of the island, with thirteen candles flaming away on top.

Everyone starts singing "Happy Birthday" . . . to me!

"Since we won't all be together next week," Tía Laura explains.

Mami sets the cake down in front of me so I can make a wish before I blow out the candles. But I can only think of one thing I really want, which I can't get. Maybe Mami can tell what I'm wishing for because she puts her hand around my shoulders and whispers in my ear, "If you want, save the wish for later," which seems like a good idea, since I can't think straight with sixteen people telling me to hurry before the candles melt down into the cake.

"So, now can we go out?" Yo asks as soon as we're done with the cake. The snow has been falling steadily since we came indoors.

Tía Laura shakes her head. "You have to finish your digestion first."

I can't believe Tía Laura has gotten even more strict in the United States. Snow is made of water, I feel like telling her. It's not an ocean, where you can drown if you swim right after a meal. But Mami has stressed that we are guests on our best behavior. I'm not about to remind my aunt that this is supposed to be the land of freedom.

The aunts and uncles push back their chairs and begin to tell stories. My grandmother starts off, a story about when Papi was my age. As she begins, I realize that it's a story I've heard before and my grandmother is getting a lot of the details wrong. Mami whispers that Mamita is all confused with grief, to let it be.

I keep glancing out the window, watching the snow coming down thicker and thicker. I'm so glad my first snowfall happened before I turned thirteen. I've been wanting to cram lots of things in before next week, so when I have kids, I can tell them, "By the time I was your age . . ." I'll have a lot to say: By the time I was your age, I had lived in a closet, I had survived a dictatorship, I had had two boyfriends, sort of, and . . . I had lost my father.

Tía Laura sees me looking out the window, and I think she feels bad denying me anything right now. "Okay, okay," she says, "if the mountain won't wait for Mohammed, then Mohammed better go to the mountain. Bundle up!"

Yo and Carla and Sandi and I put on our boots and coats. Little Fifi nags that she wants to go, and finally her mother gives in. Lucinda says that we're crazy *loquitas* going outdoors when it's so cold, where are our brains? Mundín shakes his head when I ask him if he wants to come along. He's listening to the Papi stories as if he's never heard them before. Tía Laura says Mundín is taking it the hardest, if you can measure stuff like that. I guess if hands are the measure, I'd have to agree. All you have to do is look down at my brother's fingernails to see what he's been doing in his spare time.

At the door, Carla slips away to the basement phone. She has an *important* call to make while her mother's at the table. I know who it is, too. She'll dial Kevin's house, and once he's on the line, hang up.

As we go out, I hear my grandfather telling the story of how he bought the land for the compound after the big hurricane of 1930. I know that story, too. How he built his house, and then each of his sons and daughters married and built theirs all around his, instead of like now, one in the Bronx, one in Miami, and a daughter in

Queens. He is explaining that the new government will be returning the compound to us, that we'll have to decide if we want to sell the property or keep it.

And then his voice is cut off abruptly by the storm door banging closed behind me.

A few days ago, Tío Pepe was in New York City with the Italian ambassador on some official business and he came out to see us at the Garcías'. Mami wept and thanked him for being so brave and helping us during a dangerous time. "My gratitude is to you," Tío Pepe bowed, "and to your children, who sacrificed a husband and a father to liberate our country."

Tío Pepe had a letter for me from Oscar. Carla was super curious, but I wouldn't show it to her. I was afraid she'd start building an elaborate Romeo-and-Juliet romance about Oscar—just as I once did. Carla is also always asking about my diary, but it still hurts too much to read it over by myself, much less share it with somebody else.

To tell the truth, I don't know how I feel about Oscar or about anything else anymore. I walk around and pretend everything's okay. Meanwhile, inside, I'm all numb, as if I had been buried in sadness and my body got free, but the rest of me is still in captivity.

In his letter, Oscar had just heard about my father. He said it was so sad. He said to remember that my father and my uncle were heroes who had liberated our country. He sounded just like his father. It made me cry all over again.

He also explained that he had tried to write to me lots of times. But up till a week ago, the dictator's family was in control and nothing but essential correspondence was being allowed out. Now they've fled, and the country is going to hold the first free elections in thirty-one years. Everyone will get a chance to vote for a president.

"All because of your father and your uncle and their friends. You must be so proud!"

Oscar had other news. He had been to Wimpy's, where he had seen Chucha. When he told her he was writing to me, she said to tell me to remember my wings. Chucha must have long-distance vision that she can see how low and sad I'm feeling. I guess I finally understand what she and Papi meant by wanting me to fly. It was like the metaphors Mrs. Brown was always talking about. To be free inside, like an uncaged bird. Then nothing, not even a dictatorship, can take away your liberty.

Oscar also said that the American School would be opening soon. Meanwhile, he and some of our classmates were back to having lessons in the old nursery room upstairs. The holes in the walls were plugged up and the shelves of books dusted off. Recently, what a surprise! Oscar found the queen of hearts bookmark in *The Swiss Family Robinson*.

"When we came back from the beach," he wrote at the end, "I could tell things had changed. Mami and Papi began eating their suppers with us, and Mami stopped putting her leftovers in a plastic bag in her lap. I still stand in the yard, though, and look up at a certain window."

I read and reread Oscar's letter alone by myself in the Garcías' bathroom with the door locked, just like in those old, sad days in hiding, writing in my diary in the Mancinis' bathroom.

The snow really is as magical as Mami said it would be, and it is falling so thickly and yet so silently that one thing doesn't seem to match the other. Everything is covered with a fluffy layer of white, like a wedding cake you don't want to cut into. The cars, the bushes, the bird feeders—even the lids on the garbage cans are wearing white hats! It's so breathlessly beautiful. This is something I don't want to forget. A brand-new world no one's had the chance to ruin yet.

And it makes you feel lighthearted, too. Sandi starts doing ballet leaps that look pretty silly in a winter coat, and Yo staggers around as though she's drunk to get a laugh out of us. I look up and hundreds of butterfly kisses rain on my face. For the first time since we heard the news, I feel as if I'm waking up from the bad dream I keep having, where I'm being buried alive as a substitute because no one can find Papi's body.

I close my eyes . . . and instead of Papi and Tío Toni walking on the beach, I see Papi sitting on the edge of my bed on a day not long ago in a place now so far away, saying, "Promise me, promise me." I shake my head to toss the memory away. Flakes of snow fly off from my hair.

"Oh, don't shake it away," Sandi pleads. "It looks so pretty, like little tiny marshmallows. Anita bonita, Anita bonita," she starts up a chant. Her sisters join in.

I smile, but I feel like crying, remembering Papi's marshmallow crown that Mami reminded me about when we were in hiding. Almost anything anyone says these days can spark a memory.

"Let's make a snowman," Fifi says, "peas, peas, peas." It's hard to resist her cute lisp, but Sandi says she has a better idea. "Let's make angels instead. They're so much prettier," she coaxes because Fifi looks cross.

Sandi explains how we have to lie down on the ground and

swing our arms and legs up and down, which sounds kind of messy, but also fun—something to put on a pre-thirteen list of things I've done.

We throw ourselves on the snow and swing like mad, and then we're all so cold, we run shrieking indoors. "You're going to catch your deathly colds!" Tía Laura scolds as she towels Fifi off. It's surprising—once you're listening for it—how often people bring up dying to try to scare you.

But now that Papi is dead, it doesn't seem so scary to die. Sometimes, I think it's scarier to be alive, especially when you feel that you'll never be as happy and carefree as when you were a little kid. But I keep remembering Chucha's dream. She saw us sprouting wings, flying up and away. It has to mean more than our coming to the United States. After all, as Chucha herself would say, what good is it to escape captivity only to be imprisoned in your own misery?

Later that night, the García girls and I sit around the bedroom we all share, talking about how much we all ate and how we're all going on diets tomorrow. Tío Carlos is back from driving two shifts of relatives to the subway, and now he's lying in bed, reading some history book that would put even an owl to sleep. Downstairs, Mami and Tía Laura and Lucinda are sitting at the kitchen table, remembering stuff that happened in the past. Mundín is taking out the garbage, and Fifi is fast asleep in the other bedroom down the hall. It amazes me that in this small house, somehow, like a puzzle, everyone actually fits in.

Carla goes up to the window that looks out over the backyard to the other backyards on the block to see if she can see *his* bedroom light. (How she knows it's Kevin's bedroom, I don't know!)

Seeing her standing there, I remember all those times when I used to look out the window hoping to see Oscar in the yard. Now I wonder if I was really in love with him or with that little square of freedom—the breeze in my hair and the sun on my skin?

"Hey, you guys." Carla points. "Come see your snow angels. Look how cute! Fifi's is so small!"

We join her at the window. Mundín must have forgotten to flick off the outdoor switch because the backyard is flooded with light.

What I see as I look down aren't angels but butterflies, the arm swings connecting to the leg swings like a pair of wings, our heads poking out in between! I'm sure if Chucha were here, she would say they are a sign. Four butterflies from Papi, reminding me to fly.

I close my eyes, but instead of making a wish, I think about Papi and Tío Toni and their friends who died to make us all free. The emptiness inside starts filling with a strong love and a brave pride.

Okay, Papi, I say, I promise I'll try.

Author's Note

I won't ever forget the day in 1960 when my parents announced that we were leaving our native country of the Dominican Republic for the United States of America. I kept asking my mother why we had to go. All she would say, in a quiet, tense voice, was "Because we're lucky."

Soon after our arrival in New York City, my parents explained why we had left our homeland in such a hurry. Many of the questions in my head began to be answered.

For over thirty years, our country had been under the bloody rule of General Trujillo. The secret police (SIM) kept tabs on everybody's doings. Public gatherings were forbidden. The least breath of resistance could bring arrest, torture, and death to you as well as your family. No one dared to disobey.

An underground movement against the dictatorship began to grow and spread throughout the country. Members met in each other's houses, trying to figure out the best way to bring down the dictatorship. My father and some of his friends and my uncle next door became involved in this movement.

Early in 1960, the SIM caught some members of the underground. Under extreme torture, they began to reveal names. My father knew that it was just a matter of time before he and his family were hauled away. Through the help of a friend, he managed to secure a fellowship for a surgery specialty in New York City. After much petitioning, the regime granted us visas to leave for the United States.

My mother was right. We were lucky to have escaped. That last year of the dictatorship was one of the bloodiest. After El Jefe was assassinated on May 30, 1961, his oldest son, who became the new dictator, took revenge on the whole country. My next-door uncle was hauled off by the SIM because of his involvement with members of the plot. For months, my cousins lived under house arrest, not knowing if their father was alive, praying and hoping for him to come home.

Even though it has been many years since those sad times, I still have moments when I wonder what life must have been like for them.

And so I decided to write a novel, imagining the life of those who stay behind, fighting for freedom. I chose to base the story on the Trujillo regime in the Dominican Republic because it was the one under which I myself had lived. But this story could have taken place in any of the many dictatorships in Nicaragua, Cuba, Chile, Haiti, Argentina, Guatemala, El Salvador, or Honduras—a sad but not uncommon occurrence in the southern half of our America not too long ago.

There is a tradition in Latin American countries known as *testimonio*. It is the responsibility of those who survive the struggle for freedom to give testimony. To tell the story in order to keep alive the memory of those who died.

Many of the most moving testimonies of the Dominican dictatorship have not been written down. I want to thank all those who offered me their stories of those painful times. I especially want to thank my cousins, Ique and Lyn and Julia María, and my Tía Rosa, for sharing their memories with me. My uncle, Tío Memé, who survived his prison experiences, often asked me if someday we couldn't write a book together. This is not the memoir he envisioned, but it is a fictional way to keep my promise. To give testimony.

In the Dominican Republic, there is also the tradition of saying thanks, *gracias*, to our patron saint, *La Virgencita de la Altagracia*. *Gracias* to *Altagracia* for helping me write down this story. And thanks for the helpers she put in my path: my editors, Andrea Cascardi and Erin Clarke; my agent, Susan Bergholz; my *compañero*, Bill Eichner.

Finally, I want to thank my next-door neighbor and friend here in Vermont, Liza Spears, who read an early version of this manuscript and offered helpful suggestions and encouragement. *Gracias*, Liza!